Love at C

A Cozy Monster Romance

S.C. PRINCIPALE

Copyright @ 2024 by S.C. Principale

The right of S.C. Principale to be identified as the author of this work has been asserted by her under the Copyright Amendment (Moral Rights) Act 2000

All rights reserved. This publication (or any part of it) may not be reproduced or transmitted, copied, stored, distributed, or otherwise made available by any person or entity (including Google, Amazon or similar organizations), in any form (electronic, digital, optical or mechanical) or by any means (photocopying, recording, scanning or otherwise) without prior written permission from the author.

This is a work of fiction. Similarities to real people, places, or events are entirely coincidental.

Cover Design: Chesswanderlust_sama

Editing: Evil Commas Editing

For questions or further information please contact: scprincipaleauthor@gmail.com

Dedication

This one goes out to all the Patreon supporters, AKA "My Fan-mi-ly" particularly EG and also AT, who supplied me with these wonderful stories based on their favorite characters and requests for new paranormal creatures to visit Pine Ridge!

Also dedicated to my wonderful husband and children, who take such great care of me and make my life a cozy, wonderful romance even in a hard world full of problems.

Introduction

Country Pines Motel lies on the outskirts of the small, paranormal-friendly town of Pine Ridge. If you blink, you'll miss it—literally.

But if you are lucky enough to catch sight of it, the perfect night awaits just beyond the door.

Love at Country Pines features monsters and their mates in the steamiest scenarios you can imagine. Stop in and discover:

A minotaur and his new bride on an overnight getaway.
A vampire, succubus, werewolf, and witch stranded by a hail storm.
A pooka stuck in his shifted form when his wife arrives.
A lonely kraken looking for love.
And so much more!

Six tales of monster romance, each with a happily ever after, await you at Country Pines!

Chapter One: Every Little Detail

Starring Milo and Libby from The Minotaur's Valentine

"But, Milo... we just got back from our honeymoon two months ago. Isn't it a little soon to need a romantic getaway?" I can't help it. Growing up poor left its mark. I struggle to accept that I get luxuries like splurging on things like nice dinners out and a beautiful vacation, or even just picking up an extra pack of cookies at the store.

Milo finishes putting out Freddy and Felix's bowls. "This was a gift certificate from my brother, and it has to be used by the end of the year. It's not a splurge. And we don't need a romantic getaway. We want one." Milo comes over and wraps his big, burly minotaur arms around me, putting his muzzle on my cheek. "Every day when you wake up next to me is my romantic fantasy, Valentine."

Ooh, this man. He knows what he's doing. With his big muscles holding me close and his soft, rich, deep voice calling me my favorite pet name? I almost call him out on using advanced weaponry against his new bride, but curiosity wins. "Country Pines? That new place at the edge of town?"

"It's not new, you just didn't notice it before. It's charmed. Only magically conversant people or benevolent supernatural beings can see it. Normal humans can usually find a place to stay wherever they go, but many magical beings can't. Country Pines offers a safe place to crash for visitors or those new in town. It helps Pine Ridge be a welcoming place, without letting in the bad elements. "

I nod. "How long would we go for? It's almost the end of the year, and my next course starts mid-January. I can't take off too much time and leave Doc short-handed."

"Just an overnight stay. The boys will be okay just for one night so Mommy and Daddy can have a night without distractions. One night in a secluded country lodge. A roaring fire. A glass of wine." Each sentence drops further down the octave until Milo's words reach a hidden spot only he can find.

I moan softly as the rumble of his voice makes my nerves flutter and blood pumps to my needy center. The last few months have been a mad rush of back-to-back events. "Mmm. Selling it."

"And... and maybe we could try something new while we're there?" Milo hints, bucking his hips against my rear.

"Sold."

COUNTRY PINES IS QUAINT, rustic, and charming. It's a travel writer's dream. He could use the whole damn thesaurus on this place. But Milo's description of a country lodge that's secluded doesn't ring true. There are six rooms in a single row. There's no office, just a slot on each door.

Milo feeds the gift certificate into the slot, and the door springs open. My mouth springs with it.

"Holy crap!" I drop my bag from my shoulder to the floor.

"Charmed in multiple ways." Milo walks in behind me and whistles as he looks around.

The room looked cozy and cute from the outside, but the inside reveals a dazzling mountain view, a crystal blue lake, a roaring fire, and a bed the size of Annapolis. "How?"

"I have no idea. There's not even a lake nearby! Whoever runs this place is a powerful sorcerer or witch. Maybe even fae."

I shiver a little. "I thought the fae were sneaky and you shouldn't trust them?" I whisper, suddenly nervous that the the walls might hear me.

Milo chuckles. "Very true. But the fae around here make good deals, and you can trust most of them. Besides, 'fae' covers a lot of territory. After all, Ardy is a Pooka, and that's technically part of the fae family."

I roll my eyes. "I can't keep track of all this stuff. I'm just trying to keep everything straight in my head for small animal anesthesia and surgery. I'll have to learn about the interwoven branches of magical folks later. Right now, I just want to learn every intimate detail of *my* family. My only family member." I tug Milo's sweatshirt collar and bring his lips to mine.

His large hands grip my hips, and his hot breath tickles my neck as he whispers, "Your only family? Not true. So many love you. And one day I'll make a new family with you if you want."

"Oh, I want. Let me get a few more college courses under my belt first," I whimper as Milo swivels us together, letting me feel how hard he is already. "Let's not worry about building a family right now. Let me concentrate on every detail of *you*." I catch his whipping tail as it flaps in excitement, pumping my hand up and down it the same way I would pump a cock.

Milo lows softly in pleasure. "Mm. Something new you have in mind? Something with every little detail?"

I blush. Milo has turned me into a sex fiend—and *he* was the shy virgin when we met!

Well, the shy melted away pretty quickly...

It's not that we're raving mad sex monsters (okay, maybe a little). It's just that he's so big, I'm so tight, and we both have so much love to give that we thought would never have an outlet. The physical combination plus the sheer volume of love and lust I have for this minotaur? It's off the charts. I would try anything with him as long as it was just the two of us (and maybe some accessories).

While his head is bent close to mine, I place a hand on each of his horns, and he gets the idea. They're my pull-up bar as he straightens up, cradling my waist. Once I'm at the right height, I wrap my legs around his middle and nuzzle my face to his soft brown cheek.

"All of my details are for you, baby. Let's try anything you want."

MY WIFE IS THE SEXIEST woman ever.

Proudly biased husband here.

"You took a night off from work for this," Libby whispers in a voice that's hot enough to burn. Her lips kiss away the burn, slow presses all over my much wider face as I wiggle her jeans down over her hips, nostrils twitching at the scent of her arousal.

"So we'd better not waste it, I know." My long tongue flicks out over Libby's bare thigh as I hoist her higher up.

"Bed. Bed now." Libby tugs my horns and leans back with a gasp.

I practically charge the bed, dropping to my knees with a grunt when Libby's back hits the mattress. Her bare calves, encased in knee-high socks with paw prints on them, fling over my shoulders as I burrow my head between her thighs.

I lick each soft, smooth inner thigh, working my way to the middle, pulling the crotch of her pale pink panties tight over her pussy to show how plump her perfect lips are, to accentuate the pillow of curls over her clit.

Libby whimpers as I grate the cloth against her clit. "Milo..."

"Yes, sweetie?" I pause with an innocent expression as if I don't know what my yummy Libby wants.

My Libby has the sweetest naughty mouth, but sometimes it takes a little while for her to warm up. I flick her nub with my tongue, tasting her through the fabric.

"Oh! Right there. Kiss me there."

"Mm, I love when you ask me to eat your pussy."

"Eat me all up, and I'll return the favor," Libby whimpers, squirming as I slip her panties off and swirl my wide tongue over her sweet, pouting slit. I delve in, catching her juices and working my tongue inside of her, knowing that it's easily the size of a cock. Well, a *human* cock.

Libby strains forward and grabs my horns, rocking her hips against my mouth, her slippery pussy sliding with my tongue, coating it. "Yesss," her single word is a long drawn-out hiss of pleasure.

We've barely even started.

MILO'S TONGUE SHOULD be bronzed. Or enterprising sex toy companies should make a vibrating, textured Minotaur-Tongue sex toy. It's long and slightly pebbled and bumpy, but incredibly flexible. Not to mention as wide as two average-sized cocks side by side.

The longer he licks me and tongue-fucks me, the more my inhibitions vanish and my mind goes to a horny babble of lust that I can only ever share with Milo, the person I know will forever love me and never judge me.

"Fuck! It's like having two cocks in me," I grunt as his tongue withdraws and slaps my clit with a single hard lick.

"Does my baby like two cocks in her?" Milo holds up two fingers, each one thick and smooth like a stuffed Italian sausage link. Both slide into my hole and start pistoning.

Wow, Libby. Doesn't that ruin actual sex for you?

If that's what you're thinking, the answer is no. Because Milo's cock is giant but squashy, so I'll be getting filled up beyond what his tongue or hands could offer. I'm lucky, and I make sure to tell him.

"I love it when you fill both my holes," I pant. "But I only love it when *you* do it."

To anyone who's afraid to try being double-stuffed, I'll tell you it's all about the partner. With Milo's cock in my pussy and either his tail or finger in my backdoor, I'm on some other transcendental plane of pure pleasure. There must be a million pleasure-inducing nerves in that thin wall between pussy and ass, and double penetration strokes all of them. Plus the immense stretching and fullness is its own kind of erotic pleasure.

And Milo's mouth—the sweetest, softest husband in the world has no shame when he's inside of me, telling me how he wants to fill me up with his cum and other deliciously dirty things.

But tonight, I'm turning the tables—at least for a few minutes.

I know what Milo wants. What we haven't gotten to try yet. "Do you want me to fill your hole? Do you want me inside of you while I suck your cock?"

Milo's hitched gasp tells me I've scored a point. I've put my fingers inside of him before but only sporadically, a spur-of-the-moment addition to sucking his cock.

"Want me to fuck you, baby? I've learned from the best." I lean up on my elbows and look down at my minotaur, his eyes wide and dreamy with lust. "I can make you feel good."

"You always make me feel good."

"I can make you feel…something new." I sit all the way up now, moaning softly when I have to give up the fullness inside of me to change positions, straddling Milo and wrapping my arms around his neck as he sits on the bed. All of him is so massive. The huge horns, the thick, muscular neck, and those wide, trusting eyes. "I'm so in love with you," I whisper. A year ago, I couldn't have said that. A year ago, keeping walls up and people away was the norm.

Then Milo burst in with two kittens, a bunch of flowers, and the perfect blend of sweetness and protectiveness. My anchor. My everything.

"I'm so in love with *you*. You know you're my dream girl, right?" Milo nuzzles into my neck as my hands dig into his shoulders.

"Mm, then let's hope I make one of your naughty dreams come true."

A YEAR AGO, THE ONLY fantasy I ever really indulged in was that I wouldn't end up alone. Then I saw Libby, and all my fantasies revolved around her.

How'd I get so lucky? She's actually mine. The ring on her finger—wait, why is she taking off the ring I put on her finger??

Libby puts her wedding ring and engagement ring on the little stand by the bed before she pushes me back onto it. I'm already sliding out of my pants, hooves kicking them to the side of the bed as my cock springs free.

My wife smiles at me, tosses her waterfall of pale blonde hair back, and licks her lips.

Precum drips out of me, thick and slippery. I can already feel her soft lips around me...

I don't have long to wait.

Libby bobs her head around me just once, sucking hard, until it feels like she might suck my eyeballs out along with my cum. They roll back in my head and I let out a completely unmanly whimper. Libby releases me and I whimper again.

"Fuck, you taste so good." Libby scrambles over to sit on my thigh, rubbing her wet, soft pussy lips to my leg, grinding her clit to me. My tail slides over and up, perching at the entrance of her sweet slit. With a practiced motion, Libby sits down on me, setting this secondary sensitive part of me alight while my cock is in her mouth. I can't imagine anything hotter than this, my tail in her pussy with her tongue teasing my slit.

And then I feel her soft, nimble fingers teasing under my heavy sack. My thighs jump and twitch, widening to her exploring touch. With a deft pump and glide, Libby collects my thick, slippery precum and rubs it on her fingers as well as my tight pucker. My chest feels tight in anticipation as she rubs the ring of muscle in a teasing circle before probing in, one slim finger, then two.

"Ohhh. Ohh, that's good."

"That's just the beginning." Libby sucks on me while she looks into my eyes, one fist pumping and squeezing me, milking the cum out of me, while the other begins to thrust between my cheeks.

My hooves churn at the edge of the bed. Libby's fingers have visited before, but they've never come to take charge, to fuck me like I fuck her.

"I've been studying anatomy." Libby nibbles my crown with soft bites that drive me wild.

"I've been coaching you." I recall a delightful game of strip poker with flashcards. I lost, big time.

"So, you, you big hunk of minotaur, are always able to hit my g-spot because there's no other option. It's like trying to park an aircraft carrier in a single-car garage when you fuck my pussy. You're bound to hit it."

"Flatterer."

"You do it so skillfully. Well, I happen to know that you have a special spot in here... deep in here."

I groan as a third finger pushes into me, stretching me. With lube, I know Libby could work her entire fist in me, but I'm not ready for that—yet.

"I told you we'd try something new. Want lube?" Libby strokes her fingers against my upper wall in a magical arc that leaves me temporarily speechless.

"How much more are you putting in?" Right now, everything feels comfortable—just full. And when she weaves her fingers against my insides, it's better than comfortable.

"As much as it takes to reach your prostate—because if I treat it right, it'll make you come over and over. They call it a p-spot orgasm. In human men, it can make them 'dry come.' Let's see how it is with minotaurs."

"Well, I— Oh. Ohhhhh. That spot. Right there." It's just at the very end of her fingertips. She grazes it with her extended middle finger, a place that sends an electric jolt of pleasure shooting through me, straight up my cock. Dry, my ass (no pun intended). I start dripping like a broken faucet.

"Ooh, baby likes?"

"Loves," I groan.

Libby gives me a wicked grin, lower lip bitten in a sensuous smile as she starts fucking me in earnest, making me puff and whimper in delight on every inward thrust. I can see sweat starting to trail down her cheek as she keeps pistoning her hips on my tail and working her arm at the elbow to push into me, fingering me. Fucking me.

I think of how vulnerable my sweet wife has been with me, taking someone much bigger and larger into her home, her heart, her bed, and her body. How she trusts me not to hurt her, even though these horns and hooves could do so much damage. I wince as I think about how my cock could hurt her, too, if she didn't relax around me, opening up and enjoying the fullness.

"Oh, sorry, too hard?" Libby catches my wince.

"No, Valentine. Perfect. I love you fucking me. I want you to give it to me as good as I give it to you." I bite my lip. Did that sound conceited? "I *do* give it to you good, right?"

Libby rolls her eyes. "You're sexy when you're humble, you horny sex god." She sticks out her tongue—and runs it along the throbbing vein along the back of my cock.

My tail swishes uncontrollably, but it's trapped in Libby's squeezing chasm. Her grasping walls and grasping mouth are enough to make me shoot like a geyser on a normal night, but now—

A slender arm seesaws to fuck me with her fingers, working in deeper, two of her fingers curved up in a perfect half-moon that rubs a spongy pearl of pleasure inside my tunnel.

"I'm gonna come on your tail. You like that, don't you? You like that my pussy just craves any part of you, tongue, fingers, tail, cock..." Libby leans forward, sweating cheek against my shaft.

"I can feel you getting so wet and tight in there, baby."

"When I do this—" Libby presses that spongy spot, and my ass tries to keep her fingers prisoner, holding on to the waves of pleasure that spiral out and up, "*you* get all tight. Is that what it feels like on your cock when I'm close?"

"God, yes." I buck down against her, and Libby pushes back. In seconds, we figure out the perfect rhythm of push, pull, curl, squeeze, and repeat. It's like nothing I've ever felt before, and I can't believe my sweet angel of a wife is so good to me, to give me this much raw, taboo enjoyment. "Why the hell doesn't every guy try this?" I curl my fist around my cock, stroking harder and more roughly than Libby does, feeling the peak rushing toward me.

"Maybe they haven't heard how good it is?" Libby shrugs with a little laugh. "Are you going to go get a t-shirt made, baby? One that says, 'My wife fucks my ass and I love it'?"

I laugh back. "Maybe only to wear in bed."

"I prefer you in nothing." Libby gyrates a rocking circle on my tail as she pushes her fingers in deep and holds them on my secret, sensitive spot, not letting up as I push and buck against her, chasing that tight, building sensation until...

It explodes. Spirals. Ricochets out of me with a harsh curse. Everything is warm and tingly—and wet. Very wet—but there's no cum pooling down my cock or coating Libby's bouncing breasts.

"Whoa."

Yeah, that's all I can say at the moment.

Libby is more articulate. "You didn't *come*-come. You're still all hard. Ooh. Harder than I've ever felt you."

I squeak and wheeze when her hand strokes me firmly. "Everything is super sensitive. Overloaded."

Libby rises off my tail and scoots up further onto my chest, cute ass waggling in the air as she lines her pussy up with my crown. "So what'll happen if I plunge my soaking wet slit down on top of you? Will that be too much?"

"Probably. I'll probably cum all over you in the first second."

Libby smiles in satisfaction. "Perfect."

I LOVE THIS HOTEL. There's nothing like pounding each other into oblivion, followed by wine in front of a roaring fire, overlooking a majestic mountain lake.

Milo eases into the hot tub next to me.

"Are you sore?" I ask.

"Tender, not sore. You?"

"Mm, my muscles know they exist, but they were happy to give their all." I still don't think I can walk farther than the bed. My thighs are like gelatin, and my arm is very happy that I'm only holding something as heavy as a glass of sweet red wine.

"You really did give it your all. I'll remember this for the rest of my life." Milo kisses my forehead.

"You make it sound like we're only going to do this once. Oh, jeez! Was it actually... not good? It seemed good!" I feel the wine wobble in my hand and hurry to put it down before we're bathing in Bordeaux.

"It was so good! But it's not fair to you. You didn't get anything out of it, physically."

I blink. I love my hubby, but he's so naive sometimes. "You're kidding me. Do you like watching me spread around your cock, moaning your name, about to come undone because of how good you're making me feel?"

"Duh! I mean, yes. Of course I do."

"Seeing you get all quivery and breathless as I fuck your ass is such a turn-on. And then getting to meet your newest piece of metal work," I wink and stroke his currently soft cock, "that was a nice bonus."

"Oh. Oh good." Milo swallows a couple of times. "I liked that. A lot. Not more than 'normal' sex, but a lot."

I blush. I can *feel* Milo blushing next to me. The kinky images in my mind are free flowing, and I wonder if he has any of them, too. "They make these toys. For guys. Toys that are safe to have inside of you—hands-free. In case you wanted something inside of you while you're inside of me." I can hardly get the words out around the wave of desire shooting through my chest. I can just picture Milo taking something much bigger than my fingers, and I imagine me putting it inside of him... Oh, God. I didn't know I was into that, but apparently I am.

"Or toys that wives can wear. If they wanted to get inside deeper and not have a sore arm the next day."

We sit in silence. "Do we do those things?" I whisper.

"The key word is *we*. I'll do anything with you, baby."

I lean on Milo's chest, loving the feel of so much muscle and the wide breadth of him curling around me. My personal fortress.

"My favorite thing is always going to be just simply making love to you, just your body and mine, feeling your arms wrap me up, your tail tickling my leg, looking into your eyes..." I swallow. Steamy turned into mushy fast.

And I'm okay with it, because if there is anyone more mushy than me—it's my hubby.

"That's always going to be my favorite, too, Libby. I hope we're married for a long, long time." Milo presses his lips to mine, neck craned to capture my mouth. "I don't think I could ever be bored with you—but leaving the door open to always try new things will make sure you're never bored with me."

This guy. Literally hung like a bull, loves to lick me, can fuck both my holes at once, and he's obsessed with making sure I'm happy. How could I ever get bored by that? "Honey, I'm never going to get bored with you, ever. But..." My hand drifts over his chest as he slowly brings me to straddle his waist. "The more new things I find out about you and what you like only make you that much more interesting."

Milo raises his glass.

I retrieve mine.

"To a lifetime of exploring every little detail."

I clink the rim of my glass to his as I start rubbing my swollen pussy against his shaft, feeling it waking up. "To every little detail."

Chapter Two: Some-bunny To Love

Starring Ardy and Izzy from Pumpkin Spice and Speed Dating

"Honey?"

"Ardy! You're so late, I was about to call the station." Izzy jumped off the couch, clutching her heart. Being married to a cop was hard. Everyone said so.

Izzy knew Ardy was safer in Pine Ridge than in a big city, especially since he was protected by magical influences from within himself as well as from the benevolent beings of the town.

But still.

"I'm fine, sweetie. I'm just fine. Um. No. I'm not *completely* fine."

Izzy sank back down, all the bones in her legs seeming to turn to rubber. "Are you hurt?"

"No! No, no, no. I feel fine. Um. You know how my dad wanted me to make a trip home to Ireland to celebrate his birthday with him, and I said I couldn't right now?"

"Right, because we're saving to go on a trip this summer." Izzy nodded, though Ardy couldn't see her.

"Well, Dad isn't picky about using his magic, and he sees no reason that I should be. Pookas are supposed to have a dark side, after all. He said I could trick the airline into letting me on for free, and I told him no, and... yeah. He got mad at me. Told me I wasn't a true pooka, that I was a mommy's little human, and I lost my temper at him..."

"Oh, sweetie."

"The upshot is, he zapped me a good one, and I'm going to spend the night at Country Pines. I'm pretty sure everything will wear off by morning when my Dad's birthday is over. If not, I'll have Alban fix me up."

"Alban?" Alban was their brother-in-law, Izzy's sister's husband. He was a talented warlock—and a lawyer. "Fix you up legally or magically?"

"Magically. But both if this turns out to be permanent." Ardy laughed without humor, a bitter, angry snort.

"If *what* is permanent? Why aren't you coming home?" Izzy demanded.

Ardy sighed. "I'm in... I'm in the traditional Pooka form. Not my little black hare, Izzy. You wouldn't like it. You wouldn't want to see me like this. Just know I'm safe, and I'll see you in the morning. Oops. That's Alban calling me back. Of all nights for him to be at a conference in Boston... Love you, Izzy. Night."

Izzy stared at the phone in her hand as it blipped away the call.

Oh no, he doesn't. This marriage is not starting off with secrets and hiding our problems. We're not going to end up like either of our parents, especially not Ardy's mom and dad, divorcing over magical issues!

"I'M THE KEYNOTE SPEAKER at the Saturday breakfast session that wraps up the conference, but I'll be on the noon train and home by four tomorrow. Just stay calm. Maybe you can fix it yourself. You've always been able to control your shifts before."

Ardy shook his head. "He laid a really whammy on me. Something in Gaelic about the magic in his blood and my respect for my forefathers, the great Tautha Dé Danann. I think he smacked me with god-magic."

"Eesh. Then you'd better hope it wears off by tomorrow all by itself. I don't know if I can fix that! How is Izzy taking it?" Alban asked.

"I haven't gone home. I couldn't stay at the station. I didn't want to show up at your place and scare Harper and the kids."

"It can't be that bad!"

"I'm a six-foot-tall black rabbit-dude! I look like Bugs Bunny's hot cousin." Ardy looked at himself in the mirror. His human form had lengthened and turned more lean and muscular. His abdomen, which was normally slightly defined, was now sporting a six-pack. His face had become lagomorphic, with silky black ears with soft gray insides pointing and twitching all over the place, apparently receptors for his emotions.

"At least you're the *hot* cousin?" Alban offered lamely.

"Dang it, this is—Shit. Izzy's calling back. I practically hung up on her. What if she thinks I'm lying to her? What if she hates me like this? She can't see me."

"Ardy, she's your wife. This is what marriage is—best and worst of each other."

Ardy hung up and answered the incoming call, silently wondering if his extreme Pooka form was considered the best or worst of himself. He supposed it depended on who you asked.

"WHICH ROOM ARE YOU in?" Izzy stalked along the single row of rooms. Ardy's car was the only one in the lot.

"Why?"

"Because I'm here."

"You should go home, honey. I'm not comfortable with you seeing me like this."

"Too bad. Get comfy." Izzy paused in front of the only room where a soft glow came through pulled curtains. "If you don't let me in, I'm going to stand out here and freeze."

"You're so stubborn. Look, you might not be able to handle this. I don't look like myself. I look like a cartoon character—from a bad adult cartoon. Like *Who Framed Roger Rabbit* gone bad."

Izzy swallowed. "You look... *animated*?"

"No. I'm... I'm a giant rabbit-man. I'm just missing the wings on my back. I guess even my dad couldn't whip that up across an ocean."

Izzy tried to hold a picture in her mind of the mascots and costumed figures walking around theme parks. "Well. Just let me in. We'll pretend it's a costume if you want. You can still talk. Your voice sounds the same."

Ardy hesitated. "We should be able to survive one night apart, Izzy."

Anger soared up—and sank back down. "Yep. We should. We *can*. But we should also be able to survive each other in any state, whether that's if cancer takes a body part or magic takes over. You're still you. You're still my husband. I love you. And I've always liked your little bunny butt. Now let me in before I call the cops."

Ardy laughed gently in her ear. "That old gag."

"Some things never change."

There was a click, and the door swung open. Izzy stepped inside.

ARDY SLID SLOWLY AROUND from behind the door. "Please don't freak out. Don't scream."

Izzy's mouth opened and hung that way for several seconds, her eyes raking over his form from the ears on top of his head to the long feet that would no longer fit in his shoes. "Oh, honey. You weren't kidding."

"I know. I'm..." Ardy hesitated. He didn't want to call himself a freak. That would be an insult to so many of his friends in the paranormal community. No one called Milo Angelakis, a minotaur, a freak. Well, not if they were *smart*. No one called the Kane Brothers freaks when they shifted into their dragon forms, and rumor had it they weren't purely animalistic dragons, they were sentient, humanoid dragons, capable of speech and elevated thought.

Like him.

But he was a hare.

"I'm not a freak, but I'm not exactly the stuff of legend, am I? Now that you know I'm safe, can you just forget it and go home?"

Izzy shook her head, eyes squinching up in sadness. "What? No! I came out to be here *with* you so you wouldn't be alone! Marriage means you face problems together, not apart. Come here and hug me."

Ardy smiled, heart and cheeks lifting—and his ears perking up. "Really?"

"Yes, goofball." Izzy shook off her winter coat and slid easily into his arms, face cuddled into the thick, silky fur at his chest as she grinned up at him. "Doesn't this feel better?"

Ardy nodded, letting out a sigh of relief. His mother—as nice as she was—would have needed smelling salts after seeing him like this. And his father—well, he would tell him that he should be taking advantage of his fae form to get out and raise a little benevolent chaos.

Izzy just made him feel... loved. Accepted. Wanted.

"I love you," Ardy sighed into her sweet autumn red hair.

"I love you, too. Now, can we go home?"

"Sure. Unless..." *No. That idea is ridiculous. Newlyweds or not, Izzy would never, ever want to make love like this. Even if feeling her pressing up against me, rubbing her fingers through my fur feels so... new. So nice.*

"Unless what?"

"Nothing. It's just that I already paid for the room, and this place isn't exactly a normal hotel. I can't get a refund. Cops and preschool teachers don't make much. It'd be a shame to waste it. Look. King-size bed. All the channels. The mini bar is included..." Ardy wheedled. They didn't need to make love to have fun.

"The mini bar is included? No way! And king-size? Try *King Kong*-size!" Izzy ran to the bed and bounced, flying several feet off of it when her knees hit the middle. "It's nice and cushy, too. Very bouncy!"

Ardy nodded, swallowing hard as he watched Izzy's grapefruit-sized breasts bounce and keep bouncing as she clawed at the mattress, grounding herself on the ultra-springy bed. Some of her hair came out of her ponytail, fanning out around her face.

Of all nights for his selfish father to do this—the Friday after he'd had two late nights, and Izzy had just gotten over the cold one of her students had so kindly shared. Even though they hadn't discussed it, Ardy had planned to make tonight all about togetherness. Take out, a comedy on the couch—a comedy they could ignore... He sighed and smooth his hand over his head, unsettled by the feeling of foot-long ears under his palm. "This feels so weird."

"What?" Izzy demanded. "Your ears? They're not weird. They're lovely." She beckoned him over and he sat. Izzy's fingers stroked the silky tips. "They're so velvety. They're adorable. *You're* adorable. You are one buff bunny, okay?"

Ardy nodded, hesitating. Was it just him—or was his lovely bride of just three months' vintage giving him the come hither smile that he loved so much?

NO. NO... I SHOULDN'T be attracted to Ardy when he's like this. Right?

Well, I'd never say that to Libby Angelakis. Her husband *is a bullman (I mean, taurosapien). My hubby is suddenly half-bunny, half-human. At least in looks. He's still 100% Ardy and 50% Pooka.*

Izzy's hands stroked over Ardy's ears and down his shoulders, then trailed slowly down his chest as her brain caught up to her stirring libido. He was a luxury to touch, as soft as when he was in his giant hare form, but so much more human. "Um. I didn't kiss you hello after work. I always do that."

"Oh. Right." Ardy nodded, slowly bending down to offer her his lips. Tucked under a jutting gray nose, they were still mostly humanesque with a slight split at the top. His teeth had stayed the same, although his jaw had shortened.

It was different, but not bad. Izzy pressed her lips to his and sighed in relief.

"You could have been shot. You could have died saving someone. Or just been in a crash. A fire. A spell gone wrong." Her voice shook. "I was so panicked until I heard your voice, and I'm so—so mad at myself!" She lightly thumped her fist on his chest as she hugged him tighter.

Ardy squeezed her, rubbing his fur-covered hands down her back. "Baby, what's wrong?"

"I can't believe that even for a second I hesitated to think of you as my sexy, sweet, wonderful husband, my true love, just because your body is different. Just for a second! I mean, I could have lost you. It made me realize that I love you no matter what form you are in. And I don't mean just love you with my heart." Izzy bit her lip and pushed the words out. "I mean love you—as in make love to you."

Ardy stared, unspeaking.
"Unless that's not okay?"
God, what if he thinks that's not okay?

"It's okay with me. I didn't want to ruin our Friday night, especially since we haven't had any *special* time all week." Ardy gripped her wrist and led it to his hip. "But I also don't mind if we wait until Saturday or Sunday."

Izzy kissed him again. "I missed you all week. I think I'd rather see where the night takes us. Is your—" Her hand scooted down to his zipper and her eyes widened as she felt him already bulging under her palm. "Is this the same?"

"I honestly don't know. I haven't checked yet. I'll go get cleaned up and let you know. Why don't you get comfy and raid the mini bar?"

"Sounds good."

Izzy waited until her husband disappeared into the bathroom, and then she slid out of her clothes, stopping at her panties. She undid her hair completely and arranged it to hang over her breasts. Her nipples tightened at the thought of Ardy coming back to bed—probably all fluffed out after bathing and drying, but also...

New kink unlocked?

Am I suddenly turned on by imagining what it will be like to have Ardy pounding me in that form? "At it like rabbits" *has to originate somewhere.*

And I want to see what it's like. I'm curious.

Living in Pine Ridge, Izzy heard whispers about all sorts of unusual sexual activities and couples of all kinds. Her curiosity had been piqued almost as soon as she moved to this little town and found out her sister's neighbor was a dragon shifter—and that his wife was very, *very* happy about it.

"Is it the same?" Izzy pulled out a bottle of wine, a box of chocolates, and several pieces of fruit. This place was so well-stocked.

Must be magic...

"Um. Well... Almost. It's a little more curved in the shaft and pointed at the tip. Um. It's still me, just sort of... smoothed out. It's not small. Neither are my feet. Sheesh, I have giant jackrabbit paws."

"Well, *I* have wine, fruit, and chocolate. And I hear rabbit's feet are lucky." Izzy leaned against the doorway and waited for Ardy to emerge. She thrust out one hip to accentuate her curves.

Ardy opened the door, groaning as he rubbed himself down with one towel, another knotted around his waist. "I hope the magical properties of Country Pines extend to the plumbing. If not, they're going to have to deal with one heck of a hairball in the drain."

He stopped short, standing in a cloud of steam and staring at Izzy's creamy expanse of skin as his paws slowed their vigorous rubdown.

"Well?" Izzy put her toes out to meet Ardy's paw. "Do you feel like we'll be getting lucky?" she purred.

"I know I'm the luckiest man ever, no matter how I look." Ardy reached down and grabbed her by the waist, whisking her up in his arms. "I think I can wait on the chocolates. I already found what I want to nibble on."

With a squeal, Izzy let herself be carried back to the bed, sighing as soft kisses and softer fur pressed against her breasts and down her belly. As Ardy worked toward her thighs, she seized his ears in her fist, tugging on them gently.

"Mm. Rub your thumbs in little circles. Just like that," Ardy instructed, kissing his way to the center of Izzy's panties.

"Like this?" Izzy asked with a gasp. Soft fur brushed between her thighs and down her legs as Ardy settled between them.

He propped himself up on his elbows, face nuzzling into her crotch.

"Ooh!" Izzy pulled his ears hard as he ran his tongue around the edge of her panties before pushing them to one side.

It was still Ardy. He knew what she liked, the way she wanted lots of kisses on her outer lips, the way she wanted her clit rubbed in hard up and down strokes while he started sucking on her folds.

It just felt softer. If she closed her eyes, it was like someone was massaging her pussy with a mink mitten while also giving her oral attention.

This is going to spoil me. I still love Ardy's regular "human" attributes, but this is pretty cool. Better than cool.

Izzy gasped in disappointment when his nibbling kisses and sucks stopped, but he was just sitting up to pull her panties off.

When he rose up to his knees, taking her panties down over her ankles, Izzy saw his long, upward-curving cock emerge from the gap in his towel.

"Why don't you take that towel off, baby? Fair is fair and all of that." She wiggled her bare pussy at him, her fingers reaching down to stroke herself as her eyes studied her husband's shifted equipment.

"You sure?" Ardy asked.

"Definitely sure."

Ardy dropped his towel and came closer to her when Izzy held out her hand. Without hesitation, she wrapped her fist around him, studying the shape with her eyes and her fingers at the same time.

Ardghal's cock was slightly longer than it had been before, or maybe it was just that it didn't point straight out, but curved up like a smooth pinkish-gray banana. A thin line ran down the back, starting at a small slit at the crown and stopping just before two swollen balls covered in a cloud of soft black fur.

Izzy had to close her free hand around her breast to stop from reaching out and squeezing his balls, afraid she'd lose control and hug him like a soft stuffed toy. Instead, she kneaded her own breast, thumb rolling over her nipples as she said, "It's almost like a long, hard tongue. Not too hard. It's just... different." Izzy pumped her other hand around him, watching Ardy's eyes close and his shoulders relax. "Is this okay? This feels good?"

"It feels great. Wonderful. I was so afraid you'd... I don't know. This isn't what you signed up for. Not as advertised on the box," Ardy gave her a rueful smile and gestured to himself. "It's new to me, too. I'd seen other Pooka in this form, but I never turned into it myself. I didn't mean to spring this on you. I know you hated it when your ex pulled sudden shit on you."

"His sudden shit was dumping me after years of dating without a single word of warning. I knew you had magic. I knew you could change into a horse or a black hare. I didn't know about this, but neither did you. I love you. And I like touching you. I like this body, Ardy. Not more than the other one, but just as much. Honest."

Izzy sat up, hand leaving her breast to push off against the springy mattress. She looked into Ardy's eyes as her head neared his cock. "Can I see how you taste?"

"Uh-huh. Best wife ever," Ardy moaned as she slid her mouth gently around him and began to suck. "Ohhh, God. Best wife ever."

HE WAS GOING TO MARRY this woman. Wait. Already did that. Well, he was going to marry her again, because she was turning his nightmare into a hot new fantasy. In it, his wife was on all fours on the bed, sucking almost all eight inches into her mouth, even letting the smooth, slender tip go down her throat.

Deep throating. She was deep throating him while he alternated stroking her hair and reaching down to tease her nipples, rolling them under his soft, furry fingers.

But the urge to thrust was getting hard to ignore, and something in his brain warned him not to thrust while he was in Izzy's mouth.

His hips felt like they needed to move. Like he needed to run. But he didn't want to run, he wanted to rut, hard and fast, and possibly forever, into Izzy's sweet little snatch.

With a sudden grunt, Ardy yanked his cock out of her mouth and sprang over her. Izzy screamed, but he didn't stop to discuss it. "Need to be inside you."

Ardy came around behind her, parting her cheeks to get a good look at the hot pink tunnel he wanted to fuck. He bent his head to give her a long hard suck, ending with a smack on her puffy lips that made her moan. His fingers delved into her wet core, just for a second.

Rabbits suck at foreplay, he thought. "I need to slow down."

"No! No, you don't. Fuck me, honey!" Izzy arched back into his fingers.

"I don't feel... normal. I feel like this is going to be much harder and faster than usual, and I don't... I don't know. My hips have a mind of their own?" Ardy was aware he was "humping" Izzy's ass, cock sliding along one creamy cheek in a constant sawing motion.

"Well, if it's too hard, I'll ask you to stop."

"Nn." Ardy made one last grunt before he gave up self-control. Izzy usually liked to start off with slow, shallow thrusts, and together they would build up to harder ones at a faster tempo.

This time, his cock slid in completely in one long shove. His thighs seemed built to cushion the weight of his body and support it. He went into a modified crouch behind Izzy, wide, flat paw-like feet providing the perfect base even on the marshmallowy mattress. He grabbed her hips and hammered, his cock going so fast it was probably a blur. Not that he could see it as it was 95% in Izzy's hot, wet tunnel, and the other part was blocked by her sumptuous round cheeks.

Ardy bit his lip. He knew he was fucking her like an animal, hard, fast, and desperate, but it was difficult to think straight and slow down.

"Oh! Oh! Oh my God!" Izzy made an endless stream of short, sharp cries.

With a wrench, Ardy pulled out, feeling angry, cloudy, and confused. His sudden need to go at top speed couldn't come at the expense of his Izzy. "I'm sorry!"

"I'm not! Holy sex toy! What's happening?"

"I don't know! It just feels like I need to move at that speed and like I need to come, over and over. Like I'm in heat." Ardy recalled the werewolves he knew mentioning this phenomenon of being in rut, or heat, and the desire to mate blocking out a lot of their more articulate, reasoned responses.

"Well, I don't know, either, but I'm all for it!" Izzy looked over her shoulder and smiled. "Come on, honey bunny." She waggled her rear temptingly.

Whatever control he might have reclaimed vanished.

Ardy pushed deep inside of her, enjoying the sweet silky warmth of her slit, but the need for friction was the overwhelming force. His hips began to bounce against hers, his hands on her hips keeping them locked together and stabilizing them from falling over.

IZZY RUBBED HER CLIT frantically as Ardy pounded into her pussy at top speed, hitting all the good spots inside her so fast that it almost seemed to be a buzzing motion instead of thrusts. He must be moving so fast that he's blurry.

And I'm not complaining! It was like having the world's most accurate and articulate vibrator targeting her G-spot and clit at once. Ardy's vibrations penetrated through the upper wall of her vagina and targeted her clit like heat-seeking missiles.

"Coming!" Ardy shouted hoarsely, and Izzy felt his hips slam into her and hot cum shoot into her already soaking pussy.

And then the frantic fucking started all over again.

"What? Wait!"

"Why?" Ardy held back, but just for a second.

"You just came."

"Apparently, this form has multiple orgasm capabilities."

"Ooh." Izzy laid her head onto a pillow that she snagged from the top of the bed. "I can see that's going to work out for both of us."

She was right. In seconds, Izzy came, and her contracting, squeezing muscles seemed to force another orgasm from Ardy—and without missing a beat, he kept on fucking her.

Sloshing and slapping sounds filled the room. Izzy could feel hot streaks of juice and cum running down her thighs.

She didn't care. Her husband wasn't an animal, but some animalistic part of him had been released while he was in this form, and she was thoroughly enjoying it. "Want to see if we can hit double digits?" Izzy wheezed, aching pussy pulsing.

"I'm up for it."

"HE'S DOWN. FINALLY." Ardy collapsed onto his side, rubbing his lower abs. "I have a cramp."

Izzy said nothing, just moaned.

Ardy looked at her and then looked rapidly away. His wife was the most glorious, hottest mess he had ever seen. Her pussy gaped open, swollen and full of his cum. Her skin was bright pink from the backs of her knees to the middle of her back from where they'd been rubbing each other raw.

She was every XXX-Rated dream he'd ever had, and she loved him, even like this. If he stared for too long, he'd want to fuck her again.

"Did you make it?" Izzy finally asked. "I lost count."

"I got to ten—barely. I remember you yelling 'Fourteen!' at some point. You beat me."

"I can't move. If I move, I think I'll erupt like a really weird sex volcano." Izzy slumped forward and sprawled across the foot of the bed.

"I hope you don't have bruises."

"I will. But I'm okay with it."

"I lost a layer of fur." Ardy looked at the bed and saw tufts of silky black floating about. His abs were a downy coating of gray. "Seriously. I lost my outer coat."

"Maybe you're shifting back to human?" Izzy asked, lolling her head over to look at him.

"Oh, thank God."

Izzy nodded and reached out to take his hand. "I'm so glad."

"Me, too."

Ardy held her hand in silence. He knew Izzy well enough to know when something was on her mind, but it was taking a minute to find its way out of her mouth.

"Do you... do you think we could piss your dad off once a year?"

Ardy laughed and rolled down to join her, flinging one limp arm over her back. "I love you. I'll have to do a little research, but... I think maybe since I turned into this form once, I could do it again."

Izzy explained, eyes wide. "Not all the time. Just once a year or something like that."

"Hm. Same time, same place? One night for the bunny to meet the kitty at Country Pines?" Ardy teased, one hand lightly coming to stroke the sopping heat between her thighs.

"It's a date."

Chapter Three: I Licked It So It's Mine
Part I

Starring Janet and Calder

"Hot Tips. I love it." Janet put down the bold fuschia and black business cards that bore the name of her new nail salon and put her Jeep in gear as the light changed.

"Now, if only the business looked as good as the cards." Janet stopped her dented and dusty Jeep at the end of the street and looked at the small shop front that was her ticket to a brighter future. At the moment, it was empty, dusty, and crouched down under the weight of a late spring snow. Stepping out of the Jeep, she shivered as a gust of wind whipped her long, black-brown ponytail forward over one soft brown cheek. "You don't get March weather like this in Corpus Christi," she muttered and jangled the keys she'd picked up from Silverman First Fiduciary.

The inside of the shop had "good bones." Janet closed her eyes and stripped away the cobwebs and plaster flakes, replacing them with bright fuschia accents, sleek black chairs, and three stylist stations. Behind the boxy central room, there was a short hallway leading to a cubby-sized office and bathroom. As she turned back from exploring those two rooms, Janet held up her hands, blocking the central room in her mind's eyes. A reception area. A refreshment zone with pitchers of fancy lemon and strawberry water. Hot tea. Cookies. Yes, cookies and muffins every day.

Maybe I'd better learn to bake.

Janet shook her head. *Maybe you'd better get this place painted, polished, and the furniture set up, get someone to make your signage, design your website, run ads in the local paper for a grand opening—oh, and find a place to live. Or at least somewhere to stay tonight.*

Janet went back out to her car and retrieved a broom, a mop, rubber gloves, and cleaning supplies. First, cleaning. Then, food and shelter. If worse came to worse, she could blow up her air mattress and crash in the back room. She'd have no trouble "roughing" it, not after life on the front lines.

AFTER SEVERAL DAYS of driving and hours of cleaning, Janet's back rebelled.

No wonder. Her back was her weak spot—but also a hidden strength. An accident at the base during an advanced training exercise had caused her to receive an honorable discharge, a hefty settlement, and a solid monthly check. Her injury had shut a door on one career but opened a door to the one she had fantasized about for years. It didn't replace being able to wake up without feeling like someone had put a hot poker in her spine, but she had always been a "mind over matter" type of girl.

Janet added items to her mental to-do list. *Find a place to stay tonight. Find a pool for aqua therapy. Find a place for meditation and yoga.*

Yoga and water therapy were the only things that helped her back. Her doctor recommended massage, but Janet rebelled at the thought of letting some stranger put their hands all over her defenseless body.

We had enough of that growing up, thank you very much.

But that was a lifetime ago, Yanet. I'm not that scared little girl anymore. I'm a badass soldier. I'm not even Yanet. I'm Lt. Janet Mendez, a small business owner.

"Shit!" Big, brave (okay—short and fluffy) Janet bent to pick up a roll of paper towels and felt knives of pain stab her spine in several places at once.

Sometimes strong means surviving to fight another day. Time to lock up, find some grub, and a bed for tonight.

COUNTRY PINES?

Janet slowed down. She'd planned to drive back toward the Holiday Inn advertised along the highway, but this little place was much closer.

But who calls a motel "Country Pines"? All she could picture were those dangling air fresheners and an acre of plaid.

Janet saw the chain of single-story rooms from the road, but her eyes were overtired from eighteen-hour days of driving and an afternoon of sweeping up plaster. The building shimmered and blurred, almost hazy.

If I lose my vision on top of having two metal rods in my back, I'm going to go kick Uncle Sam in his striped backside!

But when Janet pulled into the parking area, her vision cleared. "Just tired. I hope this place has decent Wi-Fi."

Moving slowly and stiffly, Janet hobbled to the front of the motel, only to blink in surprise.

"Where's the office? Where... Where do I pay?" Janet didn't see any other cars in the parking lot, but she clearly saw the "Vacancy" sign in shimmering gold.

She blinked again and the letters were simply yellow neon.

"Sign is lit..."

Janet walked faster, her back complaining. Her finely tuned senses were screaming that something was off, but her fight or flight instinct hadn't kicked in. It was more like that distant feeling of remembering

Christmas morning, of knowing there would be presents under the tree.

Anticipation. The good kind.

What the fuck?

Janet hadn't had that feeling in a long time. Even the opening of her dream salon was a mixed blessing, meaning hours of hard work, starting over in a new town, and a hundred new chances to flop.

Letting her instincts guide her, Janet walked toward the door nearest to her car. A card reader was built into the rustic wooden wall, a glaring slap of technology in a wooded wonderland.

Janet squinted but couldn't see the prices listed anywhere. "Well... If it's crazy, I'll leave and call my bank to dispute the charge." Janet dug into her wallet and swiped her debit card.

Her phone gave an instantaneous chirp as the door popped open with a sweet trilling beep. As she eased the door open, her jaw dropped.

"Holy crap!"

The bed was the size of her first postage-stamp apartment. For a moment, she didn't care what the place charged. That bed looked like the perfect oasis for her complaining back.

Janet staggered to it, kicking the door shut behind her and wishing she hadn't as her pelvis seemed to gouge into her spine. "Shouldn't be possible," she groaned and fell onto the bed. It was the perfect density with cloud-like softness and incredible support.

This place is magical.

Janet crossed herself. Her great-grandmother had told her their family line was blessed with the ability to squint between the veils. At the age of six, Janet thought that meant Abuela Viola was nuts. Now, after several near-death escapes where she seemed to know the exact moment to turn, duck, or shout a warning, Janet believed it meant she was sensitive to the spirit world. When she'd said the words, "This place is magical" in her head, she felt the familiar whooshing rush in her ears. The instinct to duck was strong.

Gotta calm down.
Watch funny cat videos.
Janet pulled out her phone and found a notification from her bank.
Withdrawal:Fifty dollars-Pine Ridge, New York.
Wait, this room cost me fifty bucks?
That was the same rate she'd paid last night when she forced herself to stop at a fleabag motel to rest her back and get a little nap.
Janet bit her lip and forced herself to take slow, deep breaths.
So, it's cheap. They have no front office staff. Hell, they have no front office! They probably have cleaning people come in each day, and that's it. Maybe the owners do everything themselves. Yeah. Pine Ridge is a Mom-and-Pop kinda place. That's all. Things are cheap.
Janet closed her eyes, trying not to lock her jaw and grit her teeth. *Don't get all wishy-washy on me now, girl. You are seizing life by the horns—no, the balls. You grab on and don't let go until you finally get what you want out of this world. It's your turn, after all you've sacrificed.*
Janet rolled to her side with a snicker as she kicked off her sneakers.
Grab it by the balls and don't let go, huh? I kinda like that idea.
Wouldn't that be a nice part of life? Finding that this town also came with great on-street parking and a boyfriend?
Men were intimidated by her. She had a soldier's training and a survivor's instinct. Men who gave bullshit answers or questionable treatment quickly retreated or found out the hard way that her injured back didn't mean her ass-kicking abilities were diminished.
I want a big, powerful teddy bear... with big powerful equipment and nothing teddy bear-like about how he uses it, Janet thought as she drifted off to sleep.

JANET WOKE UP TO A glorious sunrise shining down on a pristine mountain lake and a sparkling river.
She sat up with a gasp.

I fell asleep in my clothes.

I slept the whole night! I didn't have any nightmares. I didn't wake up changing positions in pain.

Can I rent this place permanently?

No. You can't do that, her common sense had to butt in.

But I'm going to call in every favor people in Intelligence owe me to find out who made this mattress and where I can get one!

Janet stood up gingerly. Sitting up hadn't hurt. Standing would be a challenge.

But for the first time in over a year, her back didn't twinge. Not even a nip!

Janet took a step. Then another. She did a little running twirl and—"Shit! There it is! Hello, Pain. Oh, yeah, dumbass. You're not magically healed." Janet winced as her spine reminded her of its controlling place in her life.

The thudding of wind swept past her ears and circled her temples, senses warning her that she needed to stop using that word lightly—at least around here.

Janet swallowed and stepped into the bathroom, eager to shower yesterday's grime off of her.

WARM WATER RUSHED OVER her skin and her long, thick brown-black hair. Unbound, it reached down to the middle of her back in lustrous waves. Janet would admit (in private moments alone before the mirror) that her hair was one of her best features.

Under the warm water, her aches faded. In the steamy reflection of the mirror, her thick middle and plump, mermaid-tail thighs seemed gloriously shapely, not harbingers of cellulite and spandex to come.

"Hello, old friend," she murmured.

Water had always called to her. Her great-grandmother, Abuela Viola, had said water craved her and that her happiness and destiny were in the water.

Janet took that to mean that Abuela Viola knew living in the hottest, driest part of Texas sucked, and that was why she reluctantly allowed the family enough apron string to move to Corpus Christi.

"I'm a Scorpio. Desert predator. One touch and I sting." Janet risked a naughty smile in the mirror and clicked her teeth shut with a snap.

Do deserts crave water? Or do they like being in a permanent drought?

Janet's musings had a double meaning, one she hadn't intended to allow. Wetness from the shower pulsed over her body while damp heat trickled from between her thighs. She'd been in a drought for so long. Almost 18 months. Normally, she didn't even feel good enough to attempt dating, let alone sex.

But maybe this place will be different. It feels *different.*

She finished scrubbing her hair and wrapped herself in the thick, white, fluffy robe provided.

Not even six-thirty.

Maybe I'll go outside and walk to the lake.

CALDER LIKED THIS SORT of weather. Marina, his rusalka neighbor in the river, could stand the colder waters, but as a kraken without the power to blast out energy and create a nice warm haven, he welcomed the warmth of early spring. Okay, so even spring was chilly in Pine Ridge. But Calder knew a secret.

If he swam up the river that bordered the land where Country Pines was built, the water was always just perfect. It went with the magic of the hotel, which gave its occupants what they needed for a price exacted by a mostly unknown and benevolent fae landlord. Calder had never set tentacle inside the hotel, but then again, he had no desire to. It was nice to know that he had a few spots of refuge in the winter, and in turn, he, Marina, and a few others would always take out the dark water sprites that sometimes managed to get into the stream, and the occasional ill-intentioned grindylow or kelpie.

Maybe that was why he'd never been asked to pay a price.

"Thank you. If you want me to help with something, just give me a nudge," Calder murmured as his head broke the surface of the water.

"*Argh!*"

Calder's eyes widened, and his blue-gray skin turned to a light ash in panic.

A human!

That sounds stupid, he thought as he dove back under the water and began to swim away.

Plenty of humans could see him—but they were ones in the magical community, ones married to monsters or at least aware of their existence. He didn't recognize the woman in the white bathrobe standing on the grass, but he sure as heck knew that look.

Panic. Confusion. Terror. Disbelief. Hard to believe a face can convey so much in under two seconds, but the woman had managed it. Calder had never seen that look directed at him before, but he'd heard about it and seen it on old horror movie posters.

Most people can't see me, only the ones who can know about paranormal beings. What's the deal?

"Argh!" It was Calder's turn to let out a gargling shout underwater. Something had caught one of his long charcoal gray tentacles and was pulling on it—hard.

That shouldn't feel good.

And even if it does, I shouldn't be thinking about it right now!

Calder whipped around to find the lady in the bathrobe yanking on his tentacle with a look of fierce determination, fury in her eyes as she tried to swim upward, his tentacle ensnared in two surprisingly strong hands.

Their eyes met, and the lady opened her mouth in shock when she realized that the eyes meeting hers were intelligent and reproachful.

"Shit," Calder said with a wince.

Humans. Mouths open underwater, gasping in with surprise... Yeah. Bad combo.

The woman swam up fast, and he hesitated.

She had attacked him—kind of.

She might need help. He *had* to help her. He couldn't let a human die—well, not an innocent one.

And of course, there was one other odd consideration that Calder knew he should not have, but it was there, like a hot coal in his brain.

The woman in a white bathrobe was a misnomer. He was currently chasing a woman in tight black panties and nothing else.

CALDER BROKE THE SURFACE after her, pounding her back as the small, curvy human choked and gagged. "Geez, I'm sorry. Big misunderstanding. Don't die, okay?"

The woman shot him a poisonous glare and spat out water onto the chilly grass of the bank. "What the fuck are you?"

"Manners much?" Calder had a good mind to swim away. Maybe she'd chase him again.

Maybe she'd wrap her hands around his sensitive, neglected tentacles again, giving him feelings he hadn't experienced in years, feelings he shouldn't be thinking about just now.

"What the fuck are you, *sir*?"

Okay. He failed. Calder laughed. "I'm a kraken. Are you all human?"

The woman gasped and hastily put her arms over her breasts—not that they managed to hide them completely.

Calder tried not to stare.

"*All* human? What's that supposed to mean?"

"Nothing! Well, something. I mean, you saw me. Typically only humans with ties to the supernatural world can see creatures like me. And you're here, at Country Pines. This is a supernatural-friendly hotel. Most people can't see it."

The woman gaped at him, bobbing in the water. "Yes, I'm all human! I'm... Well, maybe I notice things. I'm observant."

Calder nodded, watching the woman put a hand to her head, then slam it back down to cover her chest.

The arm wasn't doing much, considering how large and delightfully heavy her breasts appeared.

Don't stare! Pervert!

"Uh. Are you okay? You're not going to faint, are you?" he asked, trying to focus on what truly mattered—her well-being, not her body.

But his mind couldn't help making a split-second fantasy while the woman frowned, seeming puzzled at his comment.

If she faints, I can heroically scoop her up and tenderly peer down at her, pushing her hair back from her forehead as I wait for her to open her eyes and meet my gaze—

And she smacks me, screams, and maybe kicks me. I peg her as a kicker. Definitely a puncher.

"Faint? *Faint?* Like some little helpless damsel in storybooks? Hell, no. I'm a combat veteran, buddy. I've seen a lot of things worse than a dude with extra arms. Legs. Legs or arms?"

"Um. They're multi-purpose. Sort of both. I call them tentacles." Calder waggled his tentacles lazily above and below the water. The one she had gripped seemed to have a little attitude of its own, swinging from side to side as if trying to hypnotize her into touching him again.

Again, perv much?

"What... What are you?"

"I'm a kraken. Remember?"

"No, like...How? Are you a project? Is this place a lab site?" Her eyes widened. "Oh no. I knew they granted me disability and security clearances too easily. Am I about to get whisked off in the black helicopters?"

"Lady, calm down! Krakens are ancient, offspring of Poseidon's daughters and humans."

"Poseidon? Greek god?"

"Yeah." Calder crossed his arms defensively. *Just say something about my family tree, girl. I dare you.*

"But... Wait, am I having a stroke? Did I die last night? Is this heaven? I thought I was going downstairs, frankly," the woman muttered, both hands going through her hair, scraping it back from her face with a worried look and leaving her breasts hanging bare before Calder's hungry eyes.

"I think you had a nasty shock, but it's okay. We got off on the wrong foot—er—tentacle." He stuck out his hand. "I'm Calder. Welcome to Pine Ridge."

Almost dazed, the woman grabbed it. "Janet. I'm new in town. I'm opening a nail salon. I have a card... not on me." She looked down, made a yelping sound, and scrambled back up the bank and into her robe.

"Cool! I'll spread the word. My neighbor, Marina, is always complaining about how this town needs more supernatural-friendly aestheticians. There's only one barber in town that knows the deal."

Janet gaped at him. "Wait... What? How many more krakens are there?"

"Oh, I think I'm the only one, but there are a lot of nice, *friendly* paranormal citizens here. You'll probably spot them if you stick around for a few days. Some you might not recognize, but you might sense them. Like the Silvermans at the bank, or the Kanes, who have the best landscaping business in the area and run the garden center..."

"Silvermans? At the bank?"

"Uh-huh."

"What are they?"

"Werewolves."

Janet lowered herself back down onto the bank. With a slow, deliberate movement, she reached out and dug her nails (beautifully painted, Calder noticed) into her calf. "I'm not dreaming. I mortgaged my salon from werewolves?"

"Yep."

"And I'm not dead?"

"Nope."

"You're real."

"Very."

"I touched your... your wriggly thing." Janet squirmed over the word, her eyes studying the writhing mass of tentacles below the water.

Calder blushed. He wanted her to touch a particular wriggly thing, but he couldn't very well admit that. "You sure surprised me. Most humans would run. Why didn't you?"

"Well... I... I guess I tend to take risks and run toward danger. Certain kinds, anyway. I thought I saw a monster, so... All those people who claim to see Bigfoot or a werewolf or whatever say they saw it, and then they say they were scared and ran. I thought I should get proof."

Calder's stomach tensed. "Ah. We prefer not to broadcast our existence. Are you going to tell people about Pine Ridge?"

"Why? Are you going to shut me up if I do?" Janet gave him a defiant glare, chin lifted high.

"Not like you're thinking. We'd probably just have to do a lot of damage control and make sure everyone at risk of being discovered and possibly harmed was cloaked, glamoured, and hidden until the media frenzy died down—if anyone took it seriously."

"At risk?"

"Yeah, of being hunted down and dissected." Calder snapped off the words.

"Shit, no. I don't want people hunted. I've been hunted. It's not a good time." She licked her lips.

Calder wished she hadn't. They were beautiful full, pouting lips.

"Families? Do these people have kids? Werewolf kids and kraken kids?"

"I'm single. The Silverman family is pretty big."

Janet shook her head firmly. "No one hurts a kid on my watch."

Well, dip me in pheromones, why don't you? Calder's tentacles stiffened and twitched, itching to grab the girl on the shore. She was brave, bold, courageous... Sexy as hell.

"Why are you staring at me like that?" she demanded suddenly.

"I don't get to meet new people that often. It's been interesting. You're interesting—in a good way!"

Janet smirked, then laughed. "You win the interesting contest, buddy."

One of his tentacles slipped up the shore and onto the bank, resting by her leg. He didn't force it back into the water.

"Will you die out of the water? Like, dry up or something?" Janet asked. Her hand hovered on her knee, but it was inching toward his shining gray appendage.

"I would after a day or two. I can come on land. I could live there with regular access to a shower, tub, or pool. Many of my relatives have chosen that path, but I prefer larger bodies of water."

"Gotcha. And you only appear here, at this enchanted motel?" Janet chuckled again, shaking her head as if she couldn't believe the words coming out of her mouth.

"Oh no, I can swim the whole length of the river, out to the ocean. I do sometimes. I help a couple of restaurants with their fresh-caught seafood—delivered live." He smiled and stuck up two thumbs—and four tentacles.

This time, Janet's hesitant hand didn't pause. She delicately put her palm on top of the tentacle in the grass. Stroked it. Felt its texture.

Turned it over and ran her perfect nails over his sensitive suckers. She even pressed her fingers into them, circling her fingertips around each perfect fleshy circle. In turn, his suckers held onto each digit as it penetrated him, kissing and sucking on her fingertips.

Janet's mouth hung open and her chest heaved, breathing heavy enough to attract his attention in a second of shared silence.

Calder felt like he was going to pass out. No one had ever explored him like that, and he didn't want her to stop.

"I'm sorry. I am observant and used to taking detailed field notes." Janet removed her hand, voice raspy.

Calder could breathe again. "That was fine. Very fine. Uh. Yes. Like holding hands."

Janet stared at him for a long moment. "Your speech pattern changed. Breathing rate is different. Are you struggling because you need to submerge your top half in water—or something else?"

He could lie. She wouldn't know the difference.

Except that Calder had the uncanny feeling that she would absolutely know, and he was suddenly deeply troubled by the idea of lying to this woman.

She'd be mad at me. Wouldn't trust me.

I want her to trust me.

"It's something else."

"What else?"

"Um."

"Did that hurt?" Her eyebrows went up, and her face was tense.

"No! No, no. Not at all."

His other tentacles slithered and rolled slowly, walking up the bank as if waiting for their turn to be adored.

Janet's eyes lit up, and she smiled before taking both hands and rubbing the pearly opal gray of the underside of his tentacles, rimming each sucker with her fingers, feeling the smoothness of the underside, and then raking her nails gently over the slightly scaly texture on the top.

Calder's body went limp in her touch. One part didn't follow suit. The ridged, arrow-shaped phallus at the base of his torso, hidden among his tentacles, went hard. Just like an arrow, it also aimed toward its target.

Janet.

"We should stop." Calder gently pulled his tentacles back into the water, wincing with pain at the loss of her touch, the first erotic touch he'd had in so long.

"Because I was turning you on?"

Bold, indeed. He nodded, not sure whether Janet was mocking him or simply curious, like someone poking a new device to see what the buttons did.

"Huh. Funny."

Anger warred with the aftermath of pleasure. "Why?" he asked in a tight voice.

"Because I didn't think a hot squid guy would turn me on, either."

Calder's jaw dropped. "I what now?"

"Turn me on. Make me wet? This life has used me too hard. I'm out of fucks to give. When I see something I like or something I want, I go for it, whether it's to take down a scary monster or grab the hot wet guy from the unofficial welcome wagon."

Janet leaned down over the bank, robe gaping open, and kissed him softly but firmly on the lips. "I think I'll stay here again tonight. I'm looking for a rental, but I haven't found one yet. This place is cheap, and the scenery is amazing." She raked her eyes over him playfully.

Calder slapped his chest with one of his tentacles. It left an instant welt, a sting that would heal in an hour but would immediately confirm whether or not he was dreaming. He wasn't.

He surged up, using his tentacles to lift him out of the water so that he could kiss Janet back, kissing her harder. When he stopped, he panted, "Is this a game?"

"No."

"Do you always move this fast?"

"Never."

"Not to sound ungrateful or unhappy, because I'm the opposite of both—but why?"

Janet gripped his tentacle, and it was all he could do not to moan out loud and beg her to massage him until he came. "Because I'm sick of men who can't handle me. I'm sick of men who play games and lie. I like you. I like how you talked to me. I like how you told me the truth—and I can tell when someone lies."

I knew it, Calder thought.

Janet leaned down, looked at him intensely, and then licked her tongue over his lips before kissing him deeply.

"There. I licked you, so you're mine. Be here tonight?" Janet rose to her feet and swayed on the grass.

He sank back into the water, mainly to hide the erection that was trying to get Janet's attention. "Yes, tonight sounds good. But—you said I'm yours? Are you mine?"

Janet hesitated. "We'll see after you lick *me*." She waved over her shoulder and sauntered back to the hotel.

Licking Janet.

Calder was relieved when Janet made it inside her room so he could duck under the water and let out a scream of excitement.

And take care of his throbbing erection that said it absolutely could not wait until tonight—but it would be ready to give Janet the ride of her life if the "licking" went well.

Part II

I'll have to tell him to be careful with my back.

Do I invite him in?

Do I risk public nudity? I mean, more than I did already?

Abuela Viola, if this is what you meant, I take it all back about saying you were loca. *Unless he drags me under the water and I drown. Then, we're going to have words.*

Janet pulled on clothes, her body throbbing. It was tempting to take care of the urges herself, but she resisted, wanting to share intimacy with someone else for a change. The fluttering in her pussy and the pulsing, pounding sensation under her clit told her this was going to be different—not just in the mechanics of boy parts in girl parts, but in something else. There was a sweet honesty about Calder that she felt with her never-wrong gut. There were hints of all the things she liked best, the things she'd add to the mix if she ever found a build-your-own-boyfriend kit.

Big and powerful body.

Helpful.

Sense of humor.

A little bit... meek. Not passive, just...

The memory of the feel of her fingers pushing gently into him and his pulsing kisses sucking on her skin made her shudder, and the inside of her thighs were instantly wetter. He had let her take charge and responded to it—but she had no doubt that he would set boundaries and take charge when he needed to.

All the things.

That's the term. He could be "all the things."

Janet didn't care if she was getting ahead of herself. It had been a long, lonely life of deprivation—from starvation rations on missions gone wrong to trying to live on the smallest of emotional tidbits when friends and family were in short supply.

She thought he could be more than a friend.

He could be...

Well.

All the things fit him nicely.

But "mine" was the word she liked best.

"WHY WERE YOU IN SUCH a good mood this morning? I could hear you crowing like a rooster in a henhouse harem," Marina was sunning herself in one of her favorite spots, a secluded bend by the Pine Ridge NYU campus. The rusalka fed on sexual energy (a step in the right direction from human souls and lifeforce). The campus boys were her steady diet.

"I... Uh. I met a new girl in town. Well, not a girl. Woman. Business owner. She's going to open a nail salon."

Marina squealed. "Yes! You met her? So, she's aware of the 'special' residents in town?"

"She is now. We kind of... had a skirmish."

"Skirmishes don't make you howl like a wolf in heat." Marina's puzzled frown turned into one of realization. "Oooh. Met her. You two...?"

"No! We just met!" Calder blushed, blue-gray skin turning a darker stormcloud hue. *But tonight seems perfectly reasonable.*

"You horny devil."

"Demi-semi-god, thank you."

"Oh, whatever," Marina rolled her eyes. "I'm right—and I'm jealous. Years of offering you my world-class services, and that beautiful cock will never be mine."

Calder blushed and furled his tentacles in a protective cloak around the base of his torso where his cock hid. "You know I appreciate the offer—but I'm trying to live down the family predilections for irresponsible screwing and dropping offspring left, right, and center."

"So, you're not screwing—but you're thinking this one will be one that you do screw—left, right, and center?" Marina smirked. "What makes her special?"

"Well, for one thing, when she realized what I was, she didn't run away. She plunged in and yanked on my tentacle, jerking me back to her. She wasn't afraid of me—exactly. And then we talked. I liked her. She liked me. A lot." His cheeks stayed dark and flushed.

Marina scrutinized him with an air of experience and seduction that he found unnerving.

His tentacles wriggled under her gaze, almost able to touch the raw sexual power emanating from her.

"You demi-semi-gods have a thing for powerful women who make hero babies. What is she, an Amazon?"

"She's a combat veteran with a nail salon."

Marina cackled happily, pointed teeth glinting in the sunlight as she gleefully rubbed her hands. "She's going to tie you in knots, and you're going to love it! And you're going to wrap her in your coils and make little half-hero-half-god babies, and I'm going to be Auntie Marina, okay? If it's a girl, I think Marina is a great middle name."

"You're not just jumping to conclusions, you're jumping into the stratosphere. Save that stuff for Lennox and Genesis, the guys with wings." Calder crossed his arms with a stubborn set to his jaw.

But the idea of Janet sinking down on his curving, ridged cock, taking him deep as she stretched wide around his pulsing base... He felt like he'd been on dry land for days, suddenly gasping for breath.

He pictured her rocking down on him, taking him ridge by ridge, riding the deliciously ribbed layers of cartilage that females seemed to love. Janet would hold his tentacles, letting them coil around her to support her body as he fucked her. He might seem to be the one in control, but she would be using his tentacles like reins, her small, powerful hands squeezing and stroking, leaving him mute or whimpering depending on if she stroked or probed.

"I gotta go."

Marina and Calder spoke as one, staring at each other.

"I'm going 'hunting,'" Marina explained with a sexy pout.

"I'm going back to the hotel."

"HI." CALDER WAS RECLINING on the bank, long tentacles glimmering as they lazed in the water and his perfectly sculpted torso glistening in the late afternoon sun.

Janet almost tripped and rolled down the bank. "You're early."

"I like it here." Calder smiled at her and splashed into the water, coming up on the side of the bank closest to her.

Janet almost wished he hadn't done that. She had been enjoying a good ogle, one that screamed man candy (monster candy?) while also arousing all of her curiosity.

Where is his cock? Does he have one like humans?

Is he going to fuck me with his tentacles?

The sudden thought of multiple tentacles filling her pussy, pushing into her ass, and slipping deep into her mouth took her down to the grass like a physical blow.

What if his suckers just cup my pussy, and all of them are opening and closing, sucking on me, kissing it with those soft, strong little circles?

"Janet?"

"I'm happy you're here. Location question."

"Oh, about the town?"

"No, no, the town is great. I met a bunch of nice people. I noticed some people who looked 'blurry' to me. The way this hotel looked. I'm guessing the longer I'm here, the clearer I'll see them."

"Probably. If not the town, then what location?"

"Tonight's date. Want to come ashore, sailor?" *Holy crap. Corny much?* "Or should I come down there? I don't have a swimsuit, and March isn't the best time of year for outdoor swimming in New York, but..."

"Does your room have a pool?"

"The hotel?" Janet blinked.

"No, your room. The rooms usually have what you need."

"It didn't have a pool when I left this morning. I'm in a normal-sized room, dude."

Calder smirked. "How about take out at your place? I'll have you over to mine when it's warmer."

Janet wanted to say that there would be no more of this "your place, my place" nonsense.

My kraken. Mine. Found it, so it's mine.

Oh, God, I'm a walking red flag of possessiveness and clinginess, aren't I?

Keeping her voice casual, Janet nodded. "Sure. Let's try that. Give me ten minutes to freshen up. What should we order? Italian? Chinese? Thai?"

"Anything but calamari," Calder winked and made her snort.

Shit, I like him so much. So fast.

The whooshing sound that always heralded a warning sounded in her ears, but instead of making her panic, it made her want to turn back.

Janet could hear a whisper in the invisible wind.

Water calls to you...

CALDER SMOOTHED BACK his wild blue-black hair that wanted to do its own thing. "Hi." He held out daffodils. "For you."

Janet knew they were some of the only flowers blooming this early in the spring and they were picked from the wild, not gotten from a florist, but she didn't care. She liked the old-fashioned courtliness (different from eighty percent of the guys on base who seemed to think she would fall at their feet because they knew how to lace their boots). She also liked the fact that she had a feeling that the chivalry would be mixed with mind-blowing sex.

Even if he's not good at it, there are so many pieces to please me and touch me... Wouldn't suck.

Ooh, but there would indeed be suction.

"You're smirking and not speaking." Calder called her on the fact that while her mind was racing a million miles a minute, her body was still blocking the doorway.

"Oh! Uh. Come in. Hey, did you put some kind of kraken whammy on this place? Because—" Janet stepped back and gestured to a small rectangular pool that had appeared by the panoramic view of the floor-to-ceiling windows—which also hadn't been there earlier.

"Fae-owned. Most fae use wishes and desires as barter, but I think the being who owns this place manifests what the patrons desire because a happy, healthy citizen is usually a good, upstanding citizen. And if citizens have places to make more little citizens—not that we are! But, you know. If people with supernatural needs have safe places to exist and grow families? Then the town will grow, and that'll be good."

"But why would someone do that—just for this town?"

Calder held her gaze. "Have you ever had a place where you feel totally safe?"

Janet let the door slam behind him harder than she meant to. The question caught her off-guard. And it bit, with teeth that knew just where to draw blood. "Not for a long, long time," she murmured.

"So many of us haven't, either. My guess would be that the fae who own this place, whatever they are or however many of them there are—they found safety here. This could be their end of the bargain—safety for safety. And maybe the happier others are, the happier they are. That's the kind of deal most clever fae would make."

Janet nodded slowly, making a mental note to ask if fae was just a fancy term for fairies or some sort of collective noun. A flutter of fairies would be cooler, she thought.

"I'd like to make this a place that's safe for you. Home for you." Calder moved closer, his tentacles rippling smoothly, a personal ocean.

"I hope it will be," Janet admitted with a smile. "Hey, hop in the pool, and I'll get the take-out menu up on my phone."

Calder brushed her hand lingeringly, and his tentacles briefly curled around her leg and caressed it in a way that made all of her ache at once—in the best possible way.

"I hope you won't sit on the sidelines all night," he said, voice sliding down an octave, tone hypnotic as it sank, every little sound from him creating a whirlpool of lust. "I don't usually get to swim with a friend."

Janet nodded, licking her lips and trying to get her eyes to unhaze. "I spent half my childhood near Corpus Christi, Texas. There are signs everywhere that say it's dangerous to swim alone."

Part III

Janet was used to thinking of relationships as badly balanced scales. They *should* be even and equal—although she didn't mind partners taking separate but equal leads in their areas of expertise— but past dates had taught her that most men expected her to carry all the weight while they gave her nothing but crumbs. For example, they would either talk about themselves until she was so bored she could scream, or they would be silent and let her carry the conversation. The silent men creeped her out or disappointed her, expecting a payment for their "listening skills" in the form of sex after dinner. The braggy bastards were worse. They expected sex, too, and they were more irritated when she didn't put out. How could she resist anyone so "fascinating"?

But Calder... He really *was* fascinating. His conversation was genuinely helpful and interesting as he answered her questions about the town, the locals, and his life. Calder seemed equally intrigued by her, listening and asking insightful questions as she talked about her time in the service and how she'd turned into an artist to fill her loneliness—and then turned into a nail artist to help others feel beautiful by sharing her art and her passion for detail. Janet could spot someone who made the right noises in the right places without actually listening. Calder didn't do that. His comments were specific and genuine.

Perfect.

Janet decided Calder was a ten out of ten in terms of conversation, but conversation wasn't everything she needed. There had to be physical chemistry. Was her earlier attraction to him just because he was a novelty? Janet forced herself to slow down and consider instead of diving into the pool and kissing him silly.

She stared at Calder as he told her about his family, storing up details with her ears, but gobbling him up with her eyes.

He was fascinating to watch. He was technically naked, and his nudity was different from anything she'd ever seen. Her eyes could drink in his details for hours—maybe forever. The slight scaliness of his skin caught the light when he gesticulated with his strong, graceful hands. His chest moved and rippled without any apparent effort at flexing. Maybe it was his diet? Swimming all day?

The strength of his face and his jaw. The delicacy of the slight point of his ears. The perfect polished white of his teeth and the broadness of his smile.

And that wasn't even accounting for the miraculous nest of tentacles weaving, wandering, and coiling endlessly as he floated in the pool, eating Chinese take-out.

Had he hypnotized her with his voice? Those quietly sparkling eyes? The endlessly churning tentacles that created soft waves against her ankles as she dangled her feet in the water?

Janet didn't know, nor did she care. One minute, she was explaining the difference between acrylic nails and gel, and the next, she was waist-deep in water with Calder's tentacles coiled around her legs.

"Oh! Geez, I'm sorry. Did I pull? I didn't think I pulled." Calder caught her elbows and pushed her back to the side of the pool.

"Your boys are friendly," Janet replied, breathless and unable to say more. The suckers on Calder's tentacles opened and closed against her skin, making her feel as though she was getting hundreds of kisses at once. A private fantasy had always been to have multiple men adoring her at once—but she knew she was too jealous and possessive to ever attempt that in real life. She wouldn't want the strain of keeping up so many emotional bonds, anyway.

I'm a one-man woman—but Calder has enough parts to make me feel like I'm the center of an adoration sandwich.

"They're not usually so ill-mannered," Calder smirked at her but didn't force his tentacles to uncurl. "You did pet them earlier."

"And you liked that, didn't you?" Janet asked, returning the smirk, running her nails lightly over a third tentacle that bobbed by her ankle.

Calder's shuddering breath and nod was all the answer she received. "So. Like cats. Give them what they want, and they'll curl up around your legs, huh? Does that mean you're my pet?"

The kraken stiffened, and his tentacles dropped from her as if they'd gone lifeless. Janet could see the hurt on his face and the dozens of pinkish circles on her legs from his "kisses."

"I'm not an animal. I'm no pet." Calder backed away.

Shit. Communication was *not* her most special favorite thing. Growing up, conversation had not been encouraged, especially the open and honest kind. In the military, you didn't talk back to superiors.

"I know that you're not an animal. You're an amazing person. A different sort of person. I only said that because…" Janet paused. Why had she said that?

Because I wish he'd stay with me.

Because I wish he were mine.

Just like when you see the right cat or dog at the shelter and you know that an instant bond has formed…

Can I help it if it's never, ever happened with a human before?

And definitely hasn't happened with a kraken!

"Words are not my thing. Nails are. Actions."

Calder slipped closer to her, sliding so that he was between her knees, looking into her face as she sat on the edge of the pool and he swam within it.

"I may have overreacted. I'm used to living in a world where mysterious things like supernatural beings are considered less than 'normal' people. We're not believed to exist. We stay hidden for safety. I never want to be with someone who thinks I'm not equal to her. It's one reason I've never been with a human before."

Janet nodded. "I know what it's like to feel like 'less.' Funny—no, not funny, but it's interesting that when we were talking over dinner, I was thinking how awesome it is that we were equals in conversation. I haven't had that experience before. Everything with you is so new," Janet reached for his hands, not his tentacles this time, "but feels so right. Instantly right. Like when something slots into place like—"

"Two puzzle pieces fitting together?"

"Yes! Like that. And if I hurt your feelings, I never meant to. I wanted to..." Saying *keep him* would sound wrong. It would sound like she had power and saw him as property. "Keep together. I already know that it would suck if I didn't see you anymore. Th-that's all." She coughed to cover the uncharacteristic tremor in her voice, the one that she thought time and harsh realities had beaten out of her.

"I want to see you, too. Every day. I'm clingy." Calder winked as his fingers laced firmly through hers and one tentacle rose from the water to caress her back.

Janet swallowed. She didn't like to use that word about herself. She just wanted what she wanted, and she wanted to make sure those wanted items (or people) were always within easy reach. "I like clingy... but strong enough to handle what I can throw at him."

Calder's tentacle slid from her back to wriggle under her shirt, a rippling muscular massage that made all her aches flee. "Try me," he whispered.

That was one order she could follow without complaint.

CALDER GASPED WHEN she slid from his arms into the water, still dressed in her shorts and faded pink tee. Her mouth conquered his as soon as he lifted her up, strong tentacles coiling around her waist. When she needed air, he gasped out, "You're soaking wet."

"That obvious?" Janet panted between kisses.

"Your clothes."

"Oh, those. I'm not worried. They're not staying on."

"Oh. Good. Let me help." Calder's fingers scrambled over wet fabric, racing against hers to shuck her clothing and toss it to the side.

Janet's skin was a soft brown, smooth in some places and scarred in others, just like his. Round, heavy breasts smushed into his chest, frustrating him, as he would really rather explore them, particularly the hard little pebbles he could feel on his skin. "You're so deliciously soft," he marveled. "Squeezable!"

Janet leaned into his chest as she brought her legs up around his waist, finding the part where his humanoid body became thoroughly monstrous. "I'm looking for something on you that's hard. Or... Or do tentacles do the job?"

Calder said nothing as her hand dragged over his chest, past his taut abdominal muscles, tight from hours of swimming but also from tension. If she wanted to find something hard, he'd certainly show her.

But that might end the night rather abruptly. He knew his ancestors had mated with humans—but his ancestors didn't seem to have a lot of regard for human well-being. What if his cock was too much—even for the Amazon warrior reaching through his weaving tentacles on a mission of discovery?

"Whoa."

Mission accomplished, Calder thought, wincing in pleasure as Janet's hand closed around the long, thick, ridged phallus.

"Hop up on the edge!" Janet commanded, eyes wide, one hand gripping his cock and the other slapping the edge of the pool.

"I don't need to." Calder pressed his tentacles down and let the tips touch the floor of the pool, and then he stiffened them, rising straight up so that his waist rose above the water.

"Oh, no. You need to. Remember? I need detailed field notes?"

Calder shook his head, "I think they'll have to wait. I seem to remember that you licked me and said I was yours. But it's not mutual until I return the favor—and do a good job."

JANET LET HERSELF SURRENDER, telling her curiosity to hold off in favor of pleasure. As she kissed the kraken again, her body went weightless, arms and legs suddenly supported in four cradles of charcoal gray and stormy blue tentacle. Calder's hands coasted over her body as they kissed, but his tentacles shifted, lifted, and turned, taking her out of the water and eventually raising her high enough that her mouth wasn't what the kraken was feasting on.

In sexual situations, Janet's mind always had a moment of disequilibrium. Negative flashbacks from previous bad encounters caused an internal war, and her mind looked for an escape hatch. Right now, it was wondering how advanced Calder's nervous system was, marveling over how he could use four tentacles to lift her so that she was floating on the top of the water while his body dropped down, submerging him until only his head and shoulders gleamed above the surface. Not only that, but his hands and fingers were busy, delicately stroking her plump thighs and kneading her curvy rear.

"Is this what you meant? Is this okay?" Calder nuzzled her from knees to hips, lips leaving little kisses on the way. His circular suckers mimicked him, opening and closing against her skin, overwhelming her senses as she hung weightless, just skimming the warm, soothing water.

Her shields finally dropped.

This is paradise. Heaven. I thought angels had wings, not tentacles.

"Janet? We could move to a bed. Or not do this," Calder prompted gently, taking her silence for hesitancy.

"Stopping is not an option," she sighed.

"Saying stop is always an option."

"Mmm, smart man. But I meant that I don't want you to stop. Don't you dare stop when everything feels so good," Janet moaned, head turning to rub her cheek against the tentacle that held one of her arms.

"Everything? I haven't even done anything yet. But I'll do everything you want. Tell me if there are things I shouldn't do. You mentioned your back injury—"

"This is the first time something sexual hasn't hurt in almost two years," Janet explained, eyes rolling back as another tentacle snaked over her breast and fastened hungrily onto her nipple, pulsating against it as it fondled it. "As far as limits, I don't have too many. You already hit the big one—being able to stop. I wasn't always given that option."

The tender, gentle strokes of his lips over her skin stopped suddenly.

Janet opened her eyes and swallowed.

Her friendly kraken was definitely descended from the ancient sea gods, the one they called Earthshaker.

Calder had risen back up above the water, face a mask of dark, cold fury. If his eyes suddenly shot lightning, Janet wouldn't have been surprised.

"Do they still live? Those people who didn't listen to you?"

"Some do, I'm sure," Janet shrugged as best she could. What had she said? That she wanted a teddy bear of a lover who was absolutely nothing teddy bear-like when they were in bed?

"Would you like me to see that they meet their maker sooner, rather than later?"

"I—"

"I'm not a violent person. None of us in Pine Ridge can afford to be evil in our intentions if we want to stay here."

"Good to know."

"But no one hurts my Janet and gets to walk away from it."

"Not yours—yet."

Calder's features relaxed slightly. "That's timing, not intent."

Ooh. She liked that. "If they ever come near me again, you can turn them into sushi."

"Agreed."

"You'd... You'd do that? Wouldn't you get exiled or something?"

"Would you leave with me?" Calder tilted her up so that their eyes met fully.

Her insides thudded at the raw power and protectiveness in his voice. "Yeah. I guess I would, seeing as I cost you your home."

"It wouldn't be an issue. We do not put up with evil beings in Pine Ridge, human or monster. Sometimes humans are the true monsters." He glowered, whisking her close to him, mouths rapidly meeting and fusing.

Janet shuddered, heat sweeping through her. Threats are eliminated. She understood that. She had eradicated some in her time.

Calder's mouth tore away from hers and devoured the side of her neck and slid down her shoulder, words pressed against her skin. "I'll never hurt you, Seastar. Only please you."

Protective. Passionate. Pleasurable.

I'm going to need a shirt that says, "Krakens do it better."

JANET FOUND HERSELF back on the water's surface, spread like a starfish as Calder's head pressed between her thighs. His tongue was longer and more nimble than a human's, easily parting her folds and stroking over them before his lips suckled each outer and inner lip, neglecting her clit in favor of exploring everything else first.

But when his tongue did find her pearl, she almost screamed in pleasure. Calder's mouth fastened over it and sucked greedily, while one of his tentacles slowly pushed inside of her, the tip wriggling inside her entrance.

"Fuck," she wheezed, mind swirling. *One inside me. One licking me. Others cradling me, caressing me, sucking on my nipples...* Yep, the multi-man fantasy was alive and well, but it was changing. Her team of fantasy lovers shrank to one as another of his tentacles ran between her cheeks and the tip teased her anus without going in, rimming it to stimulate her nerve endings as his other tentacle squirmed deeper inside.

Even a well-endowed male would have to stop at nine or ten inches, Janet thought between waves of pre-orgasm.

Calder's tentacles go on for so much more. Five feet? Six? Not that I could have that many in me, but... Oh God. Compared to humans, he's limitless.

"I can feel your sweet pussy squeezing me." Calder moaned in pleasure as she bore down on him. In answer, he opened and closed the muscular rings that made up his suckers as they danced inside of her tight tunnel, effectively sucking and popping against the most delicate flesh inside of her—even hitting her g-spot.

Cocks were thick and could be satisfying—but they were so one-dimensional, Janet found herself thinking, as Calder's mouth and tentacles blew all of her previous notions about pleasure out of the water. They were good for delivering bulk and friction. But Calder's tentacle was doing things to her pussy that not even the most sophisticated toy could do. It curled and stroked inside of her, forcing her walls open wider as he moved from left to right as well as surged in and out, fucking her while he left pulsing kisses all over her clit. His suckers were almost sentient. They had all bunched up and honed in on her sensitive places, multiple spots inside her vagina that she hadn't realized were so capable of receiving pleasure. Spots deep inside and just at the entrance, then high up near her cervix—Calder hit them all with coordinated attacks of his suckers opening and closing.

Her resistance—if there had been any, which there wasn't—wouldn't have stood a chance. Orgasm ripped through her like a series of mines going off in a chain reaction. Pleasure burst from her in three or four spots at once, leaving her wailing ecstatic curses as her whole body thrashed, still suspended safely in his net of muscular blue and gray.

CALDER DRANK THE FLOOD of sweet and salty juice that flowed from her pussy and coated his tentacle. "Mine?" he whispered, settling Janet up against his chest, letting his arms take over supporting her weight.

"Yep. Mine?" Janet leaned her head on his shoulder and clung to him, ribs heaving.

"Most definitely."

"You gotta get up on the edge now. Fair is fair."

"Hmmm. I love the thought of your mouth around me, Seastar, but if you're mine and I'm yours... I bet we can wait until later. Right now, I would love to have something *else* of yours wrapped around me."

Janet pushed away from him and swam weakly to the edge of the pool, which was only a few strokes away. "Come here. I need leverage if I'm going to—oh."

Calder floated effortlessly on his back, arms crossed behind his head. He spread his tentacles out in the water, making a thick fan shape that would easily support her like a living raft. His cock jutted out proudly, curving towards his stomach, a series of ridges running along the front and sides. "Come aboard?" he offered.

Janet stood next to him, eyes wide and lingering on his unique phallus.

Calder bit his lip in silence. Would she think it looked too painful? The ridges were firm but soft, meant to mesh with the grooved walls of a kraken female and them together while they mated and to ensure the best chance for offspring. "Not the usual, I know, but—"

"I like it. A lot." Janet ran a finger down the back of his cock, licking her lips as he shimmied deeper into her touch. Other fingers joined her single digit, stroking along the ridges, which fluttered and flexed, seeking the grooves they craved. "Ooh. Are these like your suckers?"

"Not exactly." Calder was finding it difficult to think as she touched him. Her warm fingers were replaced by a soft, warm tongue, licking boldly at his angular crown as her fist closed over the base of him. "Not too different?" he managed to ask as his ridges sought to fill her mouth.

Janet released him with a speculative look. "You do know that most human guys are roughly the same width all the way down, right?"

"Uh... I hadn't really asked." Calder followed her gaze and realized she was measuring him with her palm. Most of his sheath was about the size of a soda can, but the base did widen, roughly to the size of a liter bottle. "We don't have to do much," Calder soothed, fearing he sounded awkward.

"The hell we don't. I'm just mentally making my list of goals. Maybe by our six-month anniversary I'll be riding you balls deep—if I can ever find where you're hiding them," Janet told him, gripping his shoulders and swinging herself aboard his chest, pussy poised over his arrow-like tip.

"Mm. I would absolutely love that—but if it never happens, that's okay. I think I have other things to satisfy you," Calder reminded her, running a tentacle lovingly over her slick opening, pausing to swirl the very tip inside of her.

Janet looked at him intently as if deciding how much to say. When she spoke, her voice was low and thick, a sensual secret just for him. "You know how many women would love to be with you? Just for the physical aspect? You could fill them up in so many ways at once."

Calder nodded, letting the lewd images in his mind run rampant. Janet with two of his tentacles fucking her pussy, working as a team, in and out in tandem, never leaving her empty. Janet, writhing as his cock stretched her pussy and his tentacle delved deep into her ass, another sliding down her throat.

He blinked himself back to the present. "I don't care about those other women. I care about *you*. What do *you* want to do?"

"Everything you've ever thought of. Everything I've ever thought of. Starting with this." Janet leaned her elbows on his chest and brought her hips down. Her calves slid past his waist, and his tentacles instantly shifted to lift her up and give her leverage.

"You're perfect," Janet marveled, again giving him a critical, half-incredulous stare. "You knew just where to put your tentacles so I could do *this*."

Calder closed his eyes as her legs pressed into him and her pussy squelched down around him, the hottest, tightest velvet wrapping and squeezing around his eager cock. His flared ridges flexed and smoothed, expanding her walls and working themselves in deeper.

"Oh. Oh, shit. Fuck! Fuck, that's incredible." Janet dug her nails into his chest as she began to post on him, making little squeaks with each rise and fall.

His deep grunts echoed her higher-pitched cries. His ridges were unused to this method of lovemaking. A kraken female would wind her tentacles with his, binding them together, walls and ridges interlocked and pulsing together in a sweet union.

Janet was like a wild dolphin, fighting the net, taming and taunting his cock by turns, taking his ridges in deep, then forcing them out as she rose.

The friction combined with her tightness was like nothing he had ever experienced, nothing he'd ever imagined.

She's going to kill me. I can't last like this. My cock is going to explode.

"Sit on me, Water Lily, and let me fill you. Sit!" Calder begged, tentacles wrapping around her ankles and hips, holding her in a seated position as she squirmed, stuffed with his cock.

Janet's eyes widened, followed by her mouth, as his cock burrowed in deep, forcing her walls open wide and massaging her entire tunnel at once with his desperate ridges as they sought nonexistent grooves.

One of her hands swept between her legs, searching for her clit as she sat back, giving him the most delectable show—a pouting pink pussy straining around blue and gray swirls of his cock, her hole pushed to its limit as his thick sheath invaded.

"I'll do that for you," he panted, placing a tentacle tip over her clit and rapidly flexing his suckers on it.

"I'm gonna come," Janet's voice was a strained whisper, her voice narrow with surprise.

"Of course you are. I would never leave you longing," Calder promised, hands reaching for hers.

She nodded, then shook her head. Janet bit her lip as her eyes closed and her head tipped back. "Not usually this hard. Or this soon!"

"Want me to stop?"

"No! No, God, no. Never stop."

"Never stop. I'll remember that," Calder ground out, feeling tremors starting at Janet's outer thighs and turning to hard shudders that raged on his cock as she climaxed. "I'm going to come," he warned, suddenly realizing that jerking out of her would likely cause some pain. "Relax. Let me lift you off," he urged, tentacles pulling half-heartedly at her waist.

"I take the pill. You're going to come in me. And you're going to come in me *now*."

It was an order, not a request.

"Yes, darling," Calder was only too happy to obey, his muscles relaxing. Soon he'd let go. In fact, just picturing how she'd look as she slid from his cock, dripping with his seed, gaping wide from his girth...

His cock erupted in torrents, long unused muscles pumping out jet after jet of pearly cream as his body went limp with relief.

Too limp.

"Hey! The boat isn't supposed to go down with a passenger aboard!" Janet yelped as they started sinking below the water.

With an effort, Calder brought his muscles back under control and regained buoyancy, his spent lover lazing against him. She had trusted him. She knew she was safe.

He liked that. Loved that. His hand found her cheek. "Good?"

"Good is not the word. Best isn't even the word. I... I didn't even know that I could... Wow." Janet laughed and gave him a smile that was sexy and bashful all at once.

He could really make her blush... "Want to do it again?" he asked.

"What? Now? Already?" Janet's flushed face registered shock.

"All you have to do is let me see your sweet pussy full of my cum, and I'll be instantly eager to fill you again. I haven't mated in... a long, long time. And even if I had, it wouldn't matter. You are the best. Beyond the best. I never knew... I never knew sexual pleasure could feel like that," Calder admitted.

"Feel like what?" Janet asked, still resting on him.

"Felt it in my mind. My brain and my heart. Not just parts of my body," Calder explained, realizing just how true it was. It had felt effortless and connected. Before... He couldn't even remember before. Loving her had blotted it out. Before there was mere physical sensation, no different than touching himself, or perhaps worse, knowing that the kraken females were not his partners, only his convenience.

"Janet is mine," he said the words aloud, his voice drifting as bliss overwhelmed him, feeling her soft, slick muscles hugging him as he slid from her. The image left behind was just as erotic as he envisioned, restoring him to almost instant hardness.

But Janet didn't answer.

"Aren't you?" His stomach dropped, and his eyes dragged from the sight of her gaping pussy and up to her still face.

Slowly, the beauty on top of him nodded, letting her fingers trail up his torso and land gently on his cheek. "Yeah. But only on one condition."

Love shouldn't have conditions, Calder thought to himself, heart clenching. *Wait. This is love? Is this love? When did it become love?*

It becomes love when you feel like you'll stop breathing if she doesn't speak. Like you'll say yes, no matter what she asks.

"Name your terms," Calder said softly, catching her fingers and pressing them to his lips.

"You have to remember something. You were mine first."

Relief swirled around him as his tentacles swirled around her, binding her to him in a many-limbed embrace. "I can live with that!" Calder crowed, right before he kissed her.

Chapter Four: Hungering

Starring Robbie, Charlotte, Tessa, and Leo from Vampire in Vegas

"You gonna make it, Robbie?"

"Mm." My husband answers in short noises, irises bright red as he sits in the back of the big SUV. Leo, his bandmate and bestie, is driving while Leo's wife (my bestie and the best witch in the world) looks anxiously out the window.

"You should pull over," Tessa whispers, eyes darting between the thick storm clouds and her werewolf husband. It's not a full moon. We're not in any danger from Leo's bite.

But I'm in imminent danger from Robbie's. Well, not *danger*. My vampire has bitten me tons of times, and it feels amazing. But we have a strict rule about no biting in the car. Blood on the upholstery is so hard to explain and even harder to get out.

"If this storm doesn't let up, we'll stop at the first motel we see."

"It's stupid. We're magical beings. Can't we just zap ourselves home?" Robbie whines. That's not like him, but he's tired, hungry, and cranky.

I understand. Leo and Robbie were on tour this week and just got back. Tess and I picked them up from the airport in Binghamton. We'd prayed the whole drive in that their flight wouldn't be canceled because of the bad Nor'easter coming in from Boston.

Hail starts to pelt the car.

"Ugh." Robbie makes a pitiful noise and gives me the side eye. We can get a room. He can drink from me. Drink from all of us. But once he does... Then the sexual energy overwhelms us all. We don't swap partners, but over the years, ever since we shared a wild weekend in Vegas, we've shared some pretty intense experiments that toe the line pretty hard. We've all agreed, we can look but not touch.

"He's really hungry," I whisper to myself (like the wolf and vampire won't hear me).

Oh, I'm Charlotte. Part succubus. Mostly human. Happily married.

Really, *really* horny right now.

"It's been a long time since we took a weekend away. Shared a bite. Or anything else." Leo shrugs as he makes his comments. Stocky, muscular Leo is a man of few words. It's clear his wolf hovers close to the surface sometimes, a fierce animalistic presence that's usually relaxed and quiet unless threatened.

Right now, his nose twitches as he hits the wipers and turns them to full blast to combat the dense rain and hail attacking the windshield.

"Tess is in," he announces to the car's occupants in the same nonchalant voice would use to tell me he wants another sugar in his coffee.

"I'm in. So is Lottie," Robbie answers, voice dark and urgent. He grips my hand.

Yes, our husbands can smell when we're turned on. It's not fair, but I'm used to it by now.

"I'm so mad at that airline." I rub Robbie's knee and let my hand move up to his thighs, covered in thin black denim.

"Wasn't the airline. Some kid with a scooter. Who lets their kid ride a scooter through Philadelphia International?" Robbie hisses, his London accent thickening in irritation. "Rode right over my carry-on as I moved through the queue. Blood splattered everywhere. Hell of a hurry to cover it up. Had to throw out the bag in the lavatory..." He leans his head on my shoulder and sniffs in hard. "Missed two meals in a row after the first delay."

"Poor baby," I murmur, moving my long blonde hair so he can nuzzle into my pulse.

"Don't blame me. I told him we could go in the men's room and my arm was all his," Leo remarks, leaning forward over the wheel, eyes glinting yellow as he pulls his wolf-like senses to the forefront of his body. "Country Pines is just ahead. We're just about five miles from home. Push on?"

"Too dangerous!" Tess shrills.

The discussion ends. I'm glad. My pussy twitches with excitement and memories. "Good call," I praise.

"Very good." Robbie licks my neck, fangs already pricking the skin. "Next time, we drive."

"I'm telling you, exposure isn't worth the hassle. We make plenty doing clubs in NYC every weekend, and there must be a thousand we've never hit," Leo sighs, ever practical.

"There it is!" Tessa sends an arc of light out of her palm. It hits the road ahead and shines on the mysterious magical motel.

"Can't wait to get inside," Robbie murmurs into my skin, lipping and licking it.

Those words have a double meaning, and I'm thrilled about both.

THE FIRST TIME WE INVOLVED Tess and Leo in something sexual, it happened in a hotel. In Vegas. It was technically Robbie's fault. Well, not his *fault*, but he started it. See, unlike the vampires in horror stories, my Robbie is just a nice guy who happened to inherit the gene that passed on his mother's inoperable cancer. Mr. Minegold, a local vampire, saved him when all other treatments failed. Robbie is a "good vampire." He never bites anyone—anyone but me, that is.

And believe me, vampire bites do not have to hurt.

Done right, they feel like you just opened up an instant orgasm spot wherever the fangs sink in.

But every person has a "flavor" to a vampire. A scent. A bouquet that creates a taste long before blood reaches the mouth. Poor Robbie had been going around for years eating a very limited array of animal blood, donated frozen stuff, and little sips from me.

When Robbie explained how badly he was craving something different, our two best friends in the world stepped up—and then immediately had an orgasmic reaction that led to... other things.

Ever since Vegas, we've had little trips where the fangs come out and the clothes fall off. You mix a vamp, a werewolf, a powerful witch, and a part-succubus, and you get one hell of a sexual cocktail.

We have rules, of course. No one touches anyone but their partner.

But watching each other is hot. Being close and sharing suped-up sexual energy is even hotter.

The heat from those memories is turning the car into a sauna. I can't wait to see what happens this time. It's been so long, everything is going to be new again.

Maybe even different?

"I'VE DRIVEN PAST HERE so many times. Never gone in," Leo says as we wait for a break in the hail and rain.

"It's fae-owned. The rooms are supposed to have whatever you need in them."

"So I'm going to find a mini fridge full of blood bags?" Robbie groans, leg jiggling impatiently against mine.

"Hey! We're the blood bags! I mean, we're here," Tessa protests, pouting.

Robbie smiles at her and their fingers tangle over the front headrest, a sweet gesture of friendship. I'm not jealous. I think it's adorable how much Robbie loves Tessa, and their relationship has gone from "girlfriend's bestie and girlfriend's boyfriend" to just "best friend."

Leo and I have a similar bond, but we're just so different that even almost eight years of friendship doesn't mean we hang out just for fun. Still, as Tessa flashes everyone her innocent, excited grin (like we're going to go get ice cream instead of orgasms), Leo and I chuckle in unison.

"C'mon. Hangry vampire in need of willing donors. This rain isn't letting up. If the motel is as awesome as they say, we'll find hair dryers and towels inside." I lean across Robbie's lap and push open his door. He grabs my arm and flings me up over his shoulder, moving with vampiric speed.

Leo and Tess follow behind, nice and leisurely. Tessa has some sort of rain shield around them. They move in a dry bubble, smirking.

"Show-offs," Robbie mutters as we huddle near the closest room. They're all available—unless people walked here on foot. Our car is the only one in the lot.

"I think you like it when they show off," I whisper, shivering next to him.

"Not more than you do," he whispers back, the bright ruby gleam in his eye so much brighter in the dark.

This shiver isn't from cold. It's lust. I can't wait to see what we get up to this time. It's been almost a year since we had a "special weekend."

I wonder if we can turn one night into two...

THE HOTEL ROOM *has* to be enchanted. The bed gives it away. It's easily the size of my living room. It's built for four. Or even eight.

"Who told them we were coming?" Leo jokes in a deadpan voice.

"Is anyone else hungry?" Robbie asks, pacing, stripping out of his wet coat and soaked-through shirt. Ice-white muscles ripple as he stalks through the room, making my mouth water. I'll never, ever get tired of looking at that handsome hunk of husband. I'm also proud of him for thinking of others.

"Ate an ungodly expensive airport steak during delay number one," Leo reminds him.

"We snacked on the way here. You didn't, poor thing," Tessa clucks, flicking her fingers and sending a barrage of towels flying from the bathroom into our faces. One hits me in the nose. Tess catches hers artfully and dries her strawberry sunset hair, spared the worst of the rain thanks to her shield, but still damp from earlier in the evening.

"I'm the main course." I grab Robbie's shoulder and settle him on the edge of the bed.

With a smile, his hands skim up my thighs to the short black skirt I wore to welcome him home. I'm also wearing a flowing, loose floral blouse that shows off my neck and cleavage. I had hoped for some welcome home hanky-panky.

I'm getting my wish and then some.

"Sit." Robbie scoots further up the bed as he pulls me into his lap. Behind us, Leo pulls Tessa to the other side. There is a pool table's worth of space between our side and their side of the bed, but I'm throbbing with anticipation as I picture us meeting in the middle.

Robbie licks my neck and pauses at my ear. "You're all mine, aren't you?"

"Always."

"Not craving anything hairy, right?" He winks up at me.

I know he means Leo. "I like everything smooth," I whisper, fingers flexing all over the creamy, perfectly smooth muscles of his chest.

"Oh! Tonight?? Honey, no. I can't!" Tess gasps.

"Can't help it. We can get another room," Leo hisses back.

"Wait, what? What's wrong?" I rip my neck away from Robbie's mouth, and he groans.

"Um. Just... uh..." Whatever it is, Tess has turned into a tomato, her skin matching her hair.

Leo takes over. "When werewolves mate, they often mate in their shifted forms. As wolves. Kind of a big deal for a male and female werewolf. When they do that, there's an added element to sex—knotting. You know. For making new little pups." Leo shrugs like nothing is wrong, but his face is tight and his quiet voice is even quieter.

"But you're not part of a pack. It's not in your bloodline, you got bitten!" I protest.

"Exactly. So I don't have a marked mate from a 'pack' or anything like that. I have a hot human wife... who's trying to get pregnant."

"Oh! Oh, my God! You *are*??" I squeal. I ignore the heartache that stings under my joy.

I want a baby. Robbie and I both do. But vampires don't make babies—not without supernatural intervention, anyway. We know a vampire-human couple who have one child, but we also know that there is some demonic mojo in the mix on the human side. Apparently whatever succubus blood I have isn't "demon enough."

"Congrats, mate. You'll be awesome parents." Robbie beams at Tessa, still in her fluttery paisley-print dress, and Leo, who is also shirtless and kicking off his jeans.

"I hope so. The problem is, my wolf has decided to manifest a little extra support." Leo gestures to a bulge in his navy boxer briefs.

"Huh?" Robbie shakes his head, his normal irises chasing the red away.

I get it. I think. Leo has a knot. I know enough non-human species to know that knotting is common enough.

"Why didn't you say anything, man?" Robbie frowns, and I elbow him.

"Because you might be sad. About... kids."

"It's okay," I reassure softly.

"And it isn't normally a big deal. Before, like in Vegas, Leo was just your average guy."

Leo frowns. "Hey."

"Shh. I just mean the knot hasn't always been there. It isn't there all the time. Only when I'm fertile. Okay. Enough gross anatomy stuff." Tess turns away as if she's done explaining.

"It's not gross! We're happy for you. Thrilled. That's going to be Leo Robert or Tessa Charlotte, right?" Robbie's hunger pangs are temporarily pushed away with a broad smile.

"Of course!" Tessa whips around, her smile nervous. "But... knotting isn't natural to human women. It's a little intense. It hasn't been going well, even when using spells."

"Can we help?"

"Hey. Maybe they can." Leo's face brightens, then clouds. "I don't know."

"If it's private or messy or something, well... Screw it. We'll do anything for you. You know that we're a pack—even a hodgepodge non-wolf one," I soothe. "Tell us what we can do, Leo."

"Robbie's bites and all the kinky voyeur shit make Tessa relax. Well, get wetter than a waterfall, and her pussy gets softer and stretchier. She might be able to take a knot better." Leo doesn't mince words.

"I'm on biting duty. It's a win-win." Robbie reassures.

Tessa's blushing face brightens."It *could* help! And if that doesn't work, I'm going to ask Farrah Fenclan how she managed to get pregnant with twins. Her husband is a huge Orc. Maybe there's a potion I haven't heard of yet."

"I bet there's one they haven't thought to mention to you, Tess. They probably didn't think you'd need it, not knowing that Leo's wolf is so eager to help that he's causing some intertrouser issues."

"You said trousers. You've thoroughly corrupted this nice American girl," Leo huffs at British-born Robbie in mock disapproval.

"No, that would be the 'kinky voyeur shit.'" Robbie smirks as he makes air quotes.

Tessa's voice is small (and adorable). "Feed Robbie first! Everything else is secondary."

Robbie and I exchange a glance. Finding out our best friends are trying to get pregnant and maybe we can help seems a little bigger than just Robbie needing a meal—after all, he's immortal. He could go weeks without eating, and it wouldn't kill him (not that we're going to find out).

"You are a sweet unselfish girl... and you still taste like raspberries and mint. Light, quick, sharp—and going to make one hell of a mum."

I smile, too.

Wish someone would tell me those words one day...

THE NIGHT HAS TURNED from mere fun to a mission. A double mission. Feed the vampire. Get Tessa wet, stretchy, and slippery.

I'm not into Leo (or Tessa, exactly) but I wouldn't mind being more hands-on sometimes. They're both so damn *pretty*. However, I think Leo might remove any stray hands that end up on his "mate."

Robbie easily recaptures my attention, a hand in my hair, forehead to mine. "You heard the witch. 'Feed Robbie first.' You don't want to mess with the most powerful witch in Pine Ridge—and possibly the East Coast."

"No, I don't." I lean back as Robbie's hand returns to its place on my leg, and this time sweeps under my skirt, tearing a hole in my nice black tights so that he can smooth his room-temperature fingers over my pussy. Two fingers slide in easily and crook forward, stroking my G-spot and rolling his thumb on my clit as his tongue swirls over my pulse.

In case you didn't know this, succubi (even part-succubi) and vampires have stupidly high sex drives. We're that couple who needs sex every day—unless we're apart. We've been apart for a week. That's like months to us. From the noises Leo and Tess are making over on their distant end of the palatial bed, I think a week apart is all they can stand, too.

"My favorite flavor. My sweet honey. Chocolate. Sex and sweetness and—" Robbie stops talking and sinks his fangs in deep as his fingers pull a knee-shaking orgasm from me.

I ride the twin waves of the bite and the orgasm, which combine into a supernova of pleasure. I would like Robbie to go on forever. Not for the first time, I wonder if this is how we'll end up staying together. If I'll eventually trade my mortality, lost in a bite—but then that means Robbie will have traded his soul by taking a human life.

Can't think of this right now. Ride the pleasure.

Sweet, pulsing pleasure as blood pumps out and Robbie works the tenderest pieces me to a frenzy, trying to turn the wet slurping sounds of his fingers inside of me into an actual stream.

As I hold onto the last little bit of reserve, he spins us on the bed, changing the view.

My eyes open and fixate on Tess and Leo. Tess is on her back, legs parted as her head hangs back off the edge of the bed. Leo is stroking that perfect pink pearl at the top of her buttercream-colored pussy lips as his cock is buried in her mouth. In the soft lighting of our room, I can see that something is different about Leo's body. I know it well. He's the only other man I've seen naked (up close and personal), after all.

My eyes linger on the organ sliding in and out of Tessa's hungry, gulping mouth. Leo's cock is an angry red and seems more swollen than usual all along the thick, sausage-like length, ending in a thick, baseball-sized swelling.

Oh. That's a knot.

Picturing petite, sweet Tessa stretched around that thing...

"Fuck!" I squeal as my pussy heaves down on Robbie's curling fingers and his other hand presses just above my pubic bone. Juice splatters in the white linen oasis between us.

"How the bloody hell are you zipping your trousers?" Robbie asks, eyes wide as he licks blood off his lips.

Leo glares briefly. "It's only when she's in heat. I mean—fertile, and it comes with the erection."

Tess pushes his thighs, and Leo backs up. With a gasp, my moon-eyed bestie sits up with a lust-drunk giggle, wiping a trail of saliva from her cheek with the heel of her palm. "It's new, definitely. Stopping the pill must've changed my hormones enough to trigger the wolf's special equipment."

Now that Leo's cock is out of her mouth, I can see that it's also longer as well as thicker. The slit on his crown is noticeably enlarged, not to mention the knot.

"Guess so," I say, trying not to stare.

I fail, of course.

"Um. I'm good. Don't need to eat more," Robbie coughs into his fist.

"What!?" Tess protests.

I know why he's hesitating. Biting others has always been fully clothed foreplay. Tess is the opposite of fully clothed, and Robbie's halfway there.

Leo makes a growling grumble but shrugs. "Just be a good little vamp and bite here." He points to the soft white skin of Tessa's arm.

Robbie shrugs and wriggles closer on the bed, his erection clearly visible through his unzipped jeans.

Tess lazily rolls toward him, arms out.

It's innocent (well, as innocent as ever), but it looks so hot to see Tess writhing and moaning as Robbie's fangs gently ease into her arm. Leo lies beside her, his hand rubbing through her curls, fingers slipping inside of her.

"Lottie's lonely," Robbie says in a thick voice, taking a break between swallows of blood.

"Then tell her to get her clothes off and get in here," Tess sing-songs, riding the high of the bite and whatever Leo's fingers are doing.

Before anyone can change their minds, I slip off my shirt and wiggle out of my bra, panties, and ripped winter tights.

Tess moans and hugs Robbie's head as he feeds.

Leo and I exchange a look. Is that crossing a line? Her soft little B-cups are pressed to Robbie. One of her hands rakes through his dark brown hair while the other reaches down to guide Leo's hand as it delves into her pussy.

But no one protests about this new level of touching.

I wriggle into the only available spot, in the gap between Leo and Tess. For a second, Leo rubs my back. My body goes all tight and hot. The gesture is friendly, but the adrenaline of multiple people touching my naked body sends prickles of arousal over me.

"Think she needs to come a lot, first, but also just to be distracted. She keeps beating herself up that it's not working. That I've changed in response to her body. For not being a wolf instead of a witch." Leo's chin is on my shoulder as he whispers in my ear.

"Maybe if you started while Robbie was still biting?" I whisper back.

"What will you do? Can't leave you with a blank space on your dance card," Leo teases with a tiny smirk.

I turn, shivering as my bare breasts brush his shoulder. Both of us gasp in, bodies tight. Behind me, Robbie growls, but Tessa kneads his shoulder, moaning softly. "More, Robbie. Please, a little more? You're only taking tiny sips."

"Anything for you, Tess." Robbie murmurs, but his eyes are on Leo and me. His hand slowly comes down to lift his perfect, beautiful cock. His hand wraps around it, stroking as he looks at my body while his fangs are in Tessa's arm.

There's an odd, tense moment. Then, Leo guides my hand slowly, shakily to Tessa's soft breasts, pressing my fingers tight around her hard nipple. "Why don't you work on this zone while Robbie provides support from the flank?"

I nod, shifting so that I'm at Tessa's head, pillowing her head on my lap. She smiles up at me with a dazed look. "Hey, sweetie," I whisper.

"You have the nicest boobs. Robbie, tell Lottie she has the nicest boobs."

"Is she drunk?" Robbie stops biting to smile up at me.

"I had a couple of glasses of red wine in the bar by the airport. You better tell her!" Tess pokes Robbie in the nose.

He sighs. "Your breasts are spheres of erotic delight, my love."

(Does he always talk like that? Mostly. He's an English major and a professional proofreader. I like the wordy side!)

"I think *your* breasts are the prettiest," I whisper in a conspiratorial voice. "Why don't I give you a massage while Leo takes care of you? Okay?"

Tess moans as both of my hands begin to make firm circles on her breasts.

I can't talk. This is amazing. I get why guys love boobs so much. They're so soft, and the nipples do such wonderful things under my hands as I tease them, pulling and pinching gently. With a little moan, Tess brings her hands up under my breasts, mimicking my motions.

My pussy jumps. Robbie and Leo are watching us.

"Lucky." Leo assesses the situation as he pulls himself on top of his wife and then sits up on his knees. Another tug, and Tessa is sliding onto his lap, onto his cock.

"You're ruining my dessert." Robbie licks scarlet traces off his fangs as he loses his grip on Tessa's arm. "And you spoiled the show."

"Get your own dessert and enjoy a different show. You're not off duty—you're just repositioned." Leo's voice is a lustful growl as he surges forward, his massive member wedged in Tessa's swollen pussy. Her normally puffy pink lips are a darker coral color from the friction of their coupling.

"Want me to do backing for a change?" Robbie joins me behind Tessa. He slides an arm around me, and we lean into each other.

"The trouble with lead singers. Put 'em in as back up, and they don't know what to do." Leo winks at Robbie as he pants.

"Oi, I know what to do mate. How's our girl feeling?" Robbie nuzzles my neck as he runs a soft finger over Tessa's spine.

"She's my girl, remember?" Leo grips her hips harder and pulls her to him with a savage tug.

"It's so good. So big," Tess answers Robbie with a whimper.

"Honey, we can't do this if it hurts." Leo's hips still.

"Didn't say it *hurt*. Said it was big."

"We can make it better," I volunteer quickly.

"We can indeed. Budge up, Lottie. Tess, put your arms back, over your head. That's a love, go limp, like a rag doll."

I squish up behind the half-supine witch, my breasts pressing into her bare back, my hands going to her tight, pebbled nipples. I can feel the rhythm in her body as she works to take Leo's swollen cock. Feeling her rocking back into me as I kneel gives me that feeling I've missed, the raw sexual energy of others flowing into me. (I do have succubus genes, after all.) The only thing that could make it better is—

"So wet for me, aren't you?" Robbie fits his hips to my rear, cock smoothly plunging in until I'm sitting against his thighs.

I let out a moan that throbs with happiness. *So full. Him inside of me. Tess against me. Leo thrusting her back into me.*

Tess is the filling in our sandwich, but this is the first time I get to take a little bite.

Speaking of which...

"Not too woozy, are you?" Robbie catches Tessa's attention with an effort.

Tess shakes her head, eyes closed, face rapt in pleasure save for the little concentration wrinkles around her lips.

What's she worrying about? How to take that massive knot that's slamming against her pussy? It'd worry me, too.

"If we could just keep her from sliding back, would that help?" I direct my question to Leo.

"It's not like we can just force it in. Even with lube..."

Robbie stops as he's about to sink his fangs into Tess's arm as it falls lazily against my shoulder. "The hotel had a bed as big as a football pitch. It has to have other things you need. Maybe even potion ingredients or something."

"Then you go look, I'm busy," Leo snarls.

Robbie snarls back. "I'm also engaged, mate."

"Want me to go?" Tessa, ever helpful, asks in between short puffs of pleasured breathing.

"No!" All three of us cry.

"The things I do for friendship." Robbie yanks out of me and springs across the bed to start pulling open drawers in the bedside table and rummaging through the mini fridge and little cabinet near it.

I bury my head in Tess's shoulder, pussy fluttering and clenching in Robbie's absence.

"Poor Lottie."

"You owe me," I tease.

Tess squirms back into me and my hands shift, sliding down her ribs, then her limp arms. My hand hesitantly joins one of hers where it frantically rubs at her swollen clit under sleek gingery curls.

All that's between my skin and her pretty pussy is her fingertips.

Fuck, I can feel Leo's cock moving in and out of her. Making her bulge.

Another inch or two lower and I could touch that knot as it rubs against her, trying to get in.

Robbie, hurry up!

"Okay, I wanna know who the hell owns this place." Robbie is suddenly back on the bed, carrying an enormous liter-size bottle bearing a label in some strange sort of script. "Tess. Bring your big brain over here and read this for me."

Tess opens her eyes and squints at the script. "It's High Celtic Fae. 'Pleasure Enhancing Lubricant, Specially Formulated for Interspecies Delight.'"

"There's also a bunch of loose-leaf tea in a blue tin called Knotting Tea. I put the coffee pot on with hot water. Have you fixed up in no time."

Leo takes the bottle and squirts a quarter of it across Tessa's pussy and his cock where they join, getting some on my fingertips, too.

It's like matter has lost all its surface tension. Leo's next thrust pile drives Tess into me, and my fingers skid down, touching her clit and making her cry out, "Yes!"

Leo stills for a second. "Do it again. If it's okay."

"If what's okay?" Robbie asks from over by the coffee maker.

"My hand slipped. Touched Tessa in an intimate spot."

"But it feels really good to have someone doing something pleasurable to combat the—the not-so-pleasurable part." Tess gives me pleading eyes.

Leo stays still. "You said it didn't hurt."

"It isn't pain, but it's not comfortable. But I bet it *will* be pleasurable once you're in, baby. I want to feel you stretching me out and filling me up."

Who am I to stand in the way of my best friend's dreams of being a parent? If only *all* noble desires came with a side of sex...

My fingers revel in touching the forbidden fruit. So soft. So slippery. My hand totally bumps against Leo's knot, and he bites his lip. We don't say anything out loud, and I don't know if Tess notices. Experimentally, I spread my fingers over her delectably full outer lips and spread them. Maybe if she was just a little wider the knot would—

"Oh, God. Oh, God, honey, I'm gonna come," Tess suddenly grabs my arm and Leo's shoulder.

"Gonna make you come a lot more once you're spread around my knot and my cock is buried in you. Do you like that big wolf cock, sweetie?"

"Ye-eesss."

I'm impressed with Leo's dirty talk skills—and I'm on the verge of coming myself, just from holding Tess while she comes undone on her husband's shifted cock. The succubus in me feels white hot energy filling my insides—and if I don't get to have the same kind of attention Tess is having in the next thirty seconds, I'm going to explode.

(No. Really. We blew up a hot tub in Vegas.)

"Fuck! Almost there, almost there." Leo is taking advantage of Tessa's pleasure to make a final push.

"Robbie! Tea later, teeth now!" I hiss, knowing the pleasure from his bite might be what takes Tessa's last bit of resistance away.

I love my husband. He abandons making tea for our bestie and comes rushing over. With vampiric grace and skill that only he can pull off, he buries his cock in me while his fangs slide into Tessa's forearm as she desperately clutches my neck in the throes of her orgasm.

Leo is growling in frustration. From my vantage point, I can see Tess' pussy is literally bulging from the girthy cock inside of her, but the knot is still working its way in.

Kinky, erotic, intimate...

Lucky. Lucky there's something she can do for her one true love that'll give them a family.

It's instinctive, without thinking. I grab her hips and push forward like a soldier who is going to take a hill or die trying.

And maybe I shouldn't have done it.

There's a high-pitched scream and a low, hungry snarl that is definitely not all-human.

But it's followed by the most amazing, orgasmic noises in the world.

"Ohhh, Leo. Leo, that's so full. So full and so good."

"My girl. My brave, perfect, beautiful Tess." Leo grips her rear and pulls her flat to his chest, stealing her from Robbie and me.

But that's okay. They're still ours.

And Robbie's all mine.

"Give them a bit." Robbie easily maneuvers me to face him, still impaled on his cock. I cling to his chest as he carries me not just to the far end of the massive bed but to the bathroom.

"That was hot," I whisper. And it was.

"From what I know, they'll be stuck like that for an hour, give or take."

Riding a huge cock for an hour? Hello, double-digit orgasms.

"We can get front-row seats."

"Mhm." Robbie's voice is thoughtful. "You know, love, my swimmers not bein' lively doesn't mean you can't be a mum. We'll get a donor. Maybe Leo would even lend us a cup of milk."

"Ew. No. Not the idea, the analogy. You're terrible." I kiss his nose.

"But you love me."

"More than anything."

"An' I know it. I'm not insecure, beautiful. Do you want a baby?"

"More than I have words for."

"That's it, then. We'll adopt, or we'll find a donor. Okay? We'll ask Minegold if there's some sort of supernatural adoption agency we can get in touch with."

"Oh, baby! Robbie, thank you! But—I think I'd like to *carry* a baby if I could. And I want it to be yours... if we can."

Robbie shrugs. "Any child you carry is mine. Any child we adopt is mine. That's the rule when you're in love. Okay?"

"Okay. You're going to make me cry—and I don't want to cry. I want to find that pleasure-enhancing lubricant and see just what that vampire cock can do."

"Well... There's a hot tub in here." Robbie points with his chin toward the large oval tub. "Wanna see if we can have a repeat of Vegas—without blowing anything up?"

"Mm. Best welcome home *ever*."

"HEY, SWEETIE. HOW'S it going?"

Tessa takes my hand and pulls me into their townhouse. Ours is only two blocks away in the same development.

I stumble through the doorway, frowning a little. It's Wednesday night, and we have book club up at White Pines. We take turns driving and we talk on the way over and the way back, but we never come in for a chat beforehand. I wouldn't have even come to the door except Tess had stopped returning my texts a little after lunch.

"Tess?"

She still hasn't answered me.

My stomach twists. Bad news? It's been a crazy busy month with grad school and teaching. I've been a busy, exhausted wreck, and now I'm wondering if Tess is going to tell me I crossed a line that night at Country Pines. Or maybe she'll want to do things like that again, and I don't want to go any further than helpful touching.

Spirals of anxiety start sparking in my head. Did I wreck our friendship? Our marriages? *Her* marriage? Is she mad because I've been the worst bestie ever this month since I've barely been able to make time to sleep, let alone go out for coffee?

"Char. I need to show you." Tessa's voice is thick and quick.

Unreadable, even to me.

"Show me what?"

"Leo told me to wait until Friday when we're all together, but I can't. I can't sit next to you and not tell you." Her voice is a hoarse whisper. A messy, trembly whisper.

"Oh, no. Oh, God. What is it?"

Tess jams her phone into my hand. The screen has lots of words, but I have to read them three times before I can speak.

Pine Ridge OBGYN Patient Portal.
Lab Results:
HCG: 700 - Range Normal
Please contact your provider to make a follow-up appointment to discuss your lab results and discuss prenatal healthcare.

"Wait, wait! Prenatal healthcare? What's HCG? What's happening?" I look up with wide eyes.

"Pregnant. It worked! The night at the motel! It worked! I'm gonna be a mom! You're an aunt! Robbie's an uncle! We were going to tell you at dinner on Friday. I found out this afternoon and called Leo at the lab. He made me promise not to tell you until he could tell Robbie, so please, please, *please* pretend I didn't tell you."

"I promise! Well, I'll try. Sometimes he can tell something is off. Oh, Tess! This is the best thing ever!"

"I wasn't sure if I should say anything yet, but good or bad, I need you with me every step of the way."

"I am, honey! I am."

Tess and I hug, standing on the tiled floor in the entryway, whisper-squealing with excitement.

When she pulls back, her cheeks are flushed and her eyes are overflowing. "I'm so happy. Relieved. I thought maybe we would never—oh. I'm sorry, hon."

"It's okay. Robbie and I decided after I finish grad school this spring and the school year is over, we'll get serious about looking into sperm donors or adoption."

"That would be so cool! Maybe our kids can be close in age," Tess cries, stealing my hands again to squeeze as she jiggles with joy. "We graduated high school and college together, got married in the same year, and bought our first houses in the same year, and oh! Oh, I'm jumping the gun, but that would be amazing!"

"Miraculous."

WHITE PINES IS OWNED by Gloria White-Creighton, the most glamorous person (well, ghost) I know. Her estate is home to almost every big "fancy" event in Pine Ridge. Her rich ex-Wall Street tycoon of a hubby is turning it into a more formal thing, where people can book the place for conferences and weddings. But book club is always a relaxed gabfest with snacks, wine, and usually a fair amount of smutty book recommendations. All of the people who attend are citizens of Pine Ridge who know that some of the residents aren't human.

Tess and I sit next to Farrah and Madge (two members of Tessa's coven).

Madge eyes Tess up, cocks her head, and squeezes her hand with a knowing look.

Damn. How does she know?

What's more, why does she give me a huge, saucy grin and squeeze my hand, too?

(I confess, Madge creeps me out. She's short and has iron-gray hair, but I can easily envision her turning any teenager who shoplifts into a cockroach or rat.)

"We should get started!" Gloria floats down, her e-reader floating beside her. "I think everyone is here."

I look around (mainly to avoid Madge's inscrutable smile). "Wait. Sophie isn't here."

Gotta look out for members of the vampire spouse club. She's married to a vampire, too, but she was also apparently a child of a vampire and a demon. She and her husband have a little boy.

I was kind of hoping to talk to her tonight so I could ask how that happened.

Georgia Fenclan waves her hand and makes a noise for attention as her mouth is full of a chicken salad croissant. She mans the counter at the local coffee shop and knows everything that's happening in the paranormal community of Pine Ridge.

"What's up, Georgia?" Gloria asks.

"Sophie isn't coming. She and Jesse are at Country Pines for a mini 'babymoon.'"

"What the heck is that?" Mrs. Angelakis, the pretty brown minotaur across from me, asks, one hand to her furry cheek in confusion.

"Like a honeymoon, Angela! Only instead of getting some alone time to start your marriage, it's where a couple goes away to have some peace and quiet while they're waiting for their baby to arrive—some couple time! Or in Sophie's case, going to Country Pines means she's trying for Baby Number Two." Georgia ends with a smirk, and everyone nods knowingly.

Everyone but Tessa and me.

"Why? Why would they go there?" I lean over and whisper to Farrah Fenclan.

"Oh, because Jesse's a vampire, and normally I don't think he could father a child without some magical intervention. Country Pines always provides what you need. It's run by benevolent fae, you know. They won't make 'deals,' but they give gifts. I expect helping create a child for a couple is much nicer than offering a changeling. Provided, of course, that the couple is sincere in their intent and defenders of the innocents in town. No one could say that Jesse and Sophie aren't incredibly helpful and—Why, Charlotte, you've gone as pale as Gloria!"

"I need to go! Um—family emergency! Farrah, can you give Tess a lift home?"

"No, no, I'm going with you. I'll drive." Tess rises out of her seat.

We weave our way through a chorus of confused goodbyes.

"Honey. Honey! Lottie! Listen to me." Tess swings me around by the shoulders and makes me look at her as we skid to a halt on the slick curving driveway outside of the mansion's opulent entrance. "What did she say?"

"That Jesse and Sophie could get 'gifted' a child by the fae running the hotel. Because they're good and loyal and all that." I put a hand to my stomach.

"That's great! But it sounds like Sophie and Jesse went there deliberately, with the intent to make babies. When I went there, it just happened to be one of my fertile days. I didn't even know it. I mean, Leo and I were trying, but we hadn't entered the hardcore tracking phase yet. And now we don't have to. It wasn't like you and Robbie went there wanting to get pregnant. You never even mentioned it. We didn't even plan to go there!" Tess smooths a hand over my cheek, nodding her encouragement, willing me to calm down.

No dice, bestie.

I slide into the car and don't even know what to do with the words spinning in my brain.

Tessa sits next to me, in the driver's seat.

We don't move.

"Drive!" I yelp.

"Keys, Char."

"Oh." I fumble for my keys and hand them over. "You know how you said it would be great if we had kids close together? Because we do so much together? College roommates. High school besties. Maids of honor at each other's weddings..." I swallow. "Cycles synced up."

Tess idles the car and looks at me. "So... You could have been in baby-making mode?"

"That sounds like the worst video game level ever, but sure. I mean, not that it matters. Not that I check or take precautions about pregnancy. What's the point when you know it can't happen, even if you're dying for it to happen?" I press my hand to my chest this time, trying to hold my heart in place. It wants to soar.

There's a chance for us.

There's a chance it already happened.

"But you didn't go there for that. It sounds like that would need to be part of the deal," Tess says gently.

"I know. I know. But... We left you alone, and we went into the bathroom. We talked about being ready to look into starting a family, however we could make it work. We both said we wanted a baby. And then," I manage a grin, "plenty of baby-making activity happened. You and Leo might have set records for how many times you can come with a werewolf cock knotted inside of you for an hour—"

"Eleven," Tess mumbles automatically, eyes suddenly hazy. "For me. One long, long one for him."

I push on. "But that hot vampire of mine wasn't far behind."

As we slowly head toward home, Tessa's big brain comes back online. "Wait. So while you were at the hotel, you actually did say you wanted a baby?"

"Yes."

"Oh. *Oh*!"

"I know! I don't know what to do. Do I tell Robbie? Get a pregnancy test? Is it too early? Why did you get a blood test?"

"Because I'm late by a couple of days, and Leo started telling me I smelled different, in a good way."

I jump in my seat. Robbie had kissed my neck only that morning and murmured that all the stress must've done something to my hormones because I smelled slightly different.

"Weird-ass predatory husbands and their noses."

"I bought a three-pack of tests and used two, one yesterday and one today. Got the blood test today and have one left. Do you want to go to my house and pick it up?"

"Okay."

"You can't use it until tomorrow morning, though. It says first-morning urine is best."

I look at the radio's digital clock and groan. "I'm not patient enough for this."

"Figure it'll give you time to explain to Robbie," Tess suggests, patting my knee.

I swallow. He'll understand the mojo of Country Pines. Will he be thrilled? Stunned?

Heartbroken if I get his hopes up for nothing?

It's going to be a long night.

"I WONDERED HOW JESSE had a son," Robbie holds me in his lap as we stare at the unopened pregnancy test in mine.

"Now we know. At least in part."

"It's a wonder word of this doesn't get out as the ultimate long-shot fertility clinic," Robbie nuzzles my neck and pushes the test from my hand. "Bed, love. School tomorrow."

I groan. "I don't wanna go to work."

"Maybe we'll have something to celebrate in the morning, and we'll play hooky," Robbie wheedles, scooping up and carrying me to our bedroom.

"I hope so. And I think word doesn't get out because the fae that cloak that place and protect it only make it work for people with some special connection to Pine Ridge. It's like their gift to the town in exchange for the protection we deliver."

"Speaking of that, Leo and I have patrol tomorrow night."

"And dinner on Friday."

"Your brain is buzzing too hard, Lottie. You need to sleep."

"I need to pee! I haven't peed since before I went to Tessa's." I squirm when Robbie puts me down.

"Why?"

"Because Dr. Internet says the concentration of HCG is highest in urine that you've held for a while, which is why first-morning urine works well for an at-home pregnancy test."

"That's been like seven hours, Char. You'll give yourself problems. Bladder infections or something. Go to the loo."

"Hey! Hey, it's technically morning. After midnight." I race for the little box left behind.

Robbie follows me. "Honey, you... You might not get the answer you want. Just remember that you don't have to be sad. There are plenty of other ways we can make a family. Okay?"

"Best husband ever. Okay. But can I please, please, please take the test now so at least I can get some sleep? Having this hanging over my head will drive me insane."

"Go pee on a stick, sweetie. Whatever makes you happy."

MY FINGERS SHAKE SO badly that I'm not sure that I can open the box. But I can. I do. I get stuff done.

Now I just have to wait for a few minutes.

Or not.

"Robbie. Robbie!" I screech when a second line appears on the test even before I finish washing and drying my hands.

"What?" Robbie almost falls through the bathroom door as I open it. Apparently, he was leaning anxiously against it.

"It's got lines! Two lines!"

"Two means baby?"

"Two means baby!" I leap into my husband's arms and let him whirl me around as we laugh and cry and babble.

And then he puts me down, and we stare at each other in shock.

I feel wobbly. "Whoa. Two means baby."

"You're gonna be a mum. And... Oh, shit, Lottie. You and Tess are due the same date then, aren't you?"

"Oh. I guess we are."

I hug Robbie again. "Think it's too late to call them and tell them?"

"I'll dial, you screech."

I hold Robbie's hand as my eyes overflow. "Sounds like a plan."

Chapter Five: Stunning

Starring Georgie and Claire from The Orc's Christmas Romance

"WE COULD JUST STAY with your parents."

"What?" I have to bellow to make myself heard over the sounds of endless power tools.

Claire rubs her temples, her wedding ring and shiny diamond making my heart flutter. She's mine now. All mine.

"We could go to your parents' house! They have space!"

"I know!" I pick up Claire's bag and mine. "But that's not ideal. I need privacy. I'm a newlywed."

Claire blushes up at me. "The cabin?"

We spent our honeymoon in one of the remote mountain lodges my parents rent out, but it's almost an hour from town. That's too far to come into work every day, and we're keeping the coffee shop and bakery open with a reduced menu for the duration of the construction on the second floor of the expansion.

"We can't spend a whole week at a hotel. It'll be too expensive!" Claire bellows.

"Well, I can't have my wife getting migraines and lack of sleep. We could close—"

"No!"

I smile. Claire grew up with millions of dollars at her fingertips, but she has the work ethic of someone who had to fight for every cent. My face sobers. This career and marriage mean everything to her. Her father is a horrible person, and he disowned Claire for choosing baking instead of banking.

Claire sighs and grabs my wrist, leading me outside. "I think it's great that Pine Ridge has a twenty-four-hour construction company that can do most of the work at night so the business can stay open."

"The benefits of living in a town full of nocturnal creatures." I wave to the construction crew I can see on the partially completed section of the expansion. A pale, skeletal hand waves back.

"We have to compromise. We stay at a hotel for a night or two, but the rest of the time needs to be with your family or we have to tough it out," Claire says firmly. "This is already costing us a ton, and I can't handle the guilt of spending even more when we have a perfectly good apartment—with a perfectly good bed." She gives me a smoldering look that makes me swallow a groan.

I walk behind Claire to the van that's been my business vehicle and personal car from the beginning. My eyes are probably glowing with lust as I watch her round body moving, putting her bag in the bag. If I didn't have an audience, I'd come up behind her, grab those generous hips, and—

Claire cuts me off in mid-fantasy. "I can feel you staring."

"Do I ever do anything else when you bend over?" I ask, coming up to toss my own bag inside. When my hands are free, I grab both cheeks with a contented sigh.

"Sweetie! The construction team!" Claire hisses and giggles, squirming away. "Save it for the hotel."

"Oh, I will. Hop in." I easily lift Claire up and shoo her through the open back of the van to the passenger's seat.

Watching her climb through the empty space that's often full of freshly baked deliveries, I suddenly freeze.

I'm going to need a new car one day. This van will just be for work. I can suddenly picture Claire with our daughter by the hand and our son on her hip. I'm going to need something car-seat friendly. And then there's college to pay for. Ballet lessons. Basketball uniforms. Braces. My daughter's wedding. I'll be walking her down the aisle, a far, far better dad than Claire's ever was.

Everything swims in a rosy familial fantasy, time speeding up and slowing down in little moments that haven't even happened yet. I enjoy paddling in the sea of my happy thoughts until Claire asks, "You okay?" and I snap back to the present.

"I—uh— I'm looking for my keys."

"In your back pocket, babe."

"Oh. Yeah. Yep, right there," I pat my jeans and hear the telltale jingle. "I'll drive. And maybe you're right. We don't want to spend money where we don't have to."

"I was just going to say you were right about taking at least a night or two away," Claire sighs and settles back in the seat. When I sit beside her, she squeezes my knee in a way that sends all my blood into the direction of my groin.

"Oh?"

"We are newlyweds. We should have some time alone. Where no one can overhear us." Her hand moves up my thigh. "You said Country Pines is secluded, right? And the only other guests would be supernatural ones, so that means it won't be crowded?"

I nod, starting the van and jerking out into the street. I have to focus on driving, or I'd pull Claire into the back right now. It's not fair how she can tempt me without even trying.

That's not a complaint, it's just a very satisfied observation.

"You're growling, honey."

"I was thinking about things," I confess. "Things I'm looking forward to." I smile over her, loving the way she giggles. "Not just about tonight. About the rest of my life with you. With a family. I love you, and I love thinking about everything that's coming." I reach out and move a strand of long, chocolate-brown hair over her shoulder. "But it also makes me realize how damn lucky I am that I can get you alone and have you all to myself. I'm going to enjoy every single inch of you, Mrs. Fenclan."

I'VE BEEN WITH GEORGIE for less than a year. We met in the fall, started dating, got engaged right before Christmas, and got married in May. That sounds like a short ride, but it was jam-packed. I came to Pine Ridge alone, disowned, and almost broke, and less than a year later, I have friends, besties, adopted family, in-laws, my dream job, and my dream man. If I stop and pinch myself every day, there's a reason.

But I have to admit that I still don't understand why my husband is so obsessed with me. My body image issues (thank you, Rich Bitch Peer Pressure Club) have reared their ugly heads less and less. Georgie is honest—okay, downright blunt—with everyone, so if he loved me but didn't find me attractive, I think he'd tell me.

But that's just it. He seems to think I'm actually, factually, really truly gorgeous.

"Honey, why do you keep pinching your leg? Do you have a cramp? Should we stop and get some lotion?" Georgie flashes me a wide grin as he drives, his small tusks peeking over the edge of his lower lip. "I could massage you."

"I'm all sweaty and grungy." I know, I know. I shouldn't have said that, but it's true. Baking is hot work, and baking as a business is doubly so.

Georgie looks at me, smile disappearing. He darts his eyes back to the road. "Do you think I don't know that? We go through a bottle of shampoo a week."

"Our hair game is awesome." I reach out and gently tug the long golden blonde braid that hangs over his shoulder. He curls one damp tendril of my hair around his thick green fingers.

"You didn't answer me," he murmurs.

"About?"

"Your leg. Are you in pain?"

My big green grump is secretly a marshmallow—at least to me. "I was checking to make sure I wasn't dreaming. Things have gotten so good, so fast. You spoil me." *You're in love with me.*

It might seem silly to marvel at that but after years of feeling like no one loved me, like no one *could* because I couldn't please anyone—Georgie's fierce devotion shocks me. Surprises me.

"You think you're the lucky one?" Georgie's voice holds as much incredulity as my inner thoughts. "I never left my kitchen or my apartment. I was sure I would be alone. The day you walked into the shop—" he trails off, humming softly.

"What?"

"You might not like it."

"It can't be that bad. It's you."

"I think I've told you this before. I caught a glimpse of you?" Georgie's eyes close, and the hum turns into something low and lusty that makes me wriggle in my seat. "I promise I don't always judge a woman by how she fills out a pair of jeans, but you... Mm." He chuckles through his nose, a muted sound that makes me turn to jelly inside. "I wanted to grab hold of you from that second on."

I smile. "I can't believe that."

"But it's true. Even now, sometimes I just think of you and our future. Babies. Sitting next to you at our daughter's first dance recital or swim meet. Walking her down the aisle and taking my place next to you. Oh, God. I'm going to cry so much." Georgie groans. "It's not normal to act like this."

"You realize I'll get even more stretch marks if we have kids? And things will sag?" I touch my hair. "And go gray?"

"My mother's hair is quite gray."

"Your mother looks like a supermodel—one in her fifties, but still."

"You look like a supermodel to me! And all the bags, sags, and wrinkles will be proof we lived a life together, love of mine."

We've been driving for only a few minutes, but Pine Ridge isn't that big. We're already heading out of the town proper and into the windy mountain roads that split off from the main interstate. Country Pines isn't far.

"I don't understand how you can say that, that's all." I rub Georgie's arm. "I'm not doubting it—I'm just doubting myself, I guess. I've felt the most beautiful I ever have in my life this year."

"Probably because you were allowed to see yourself without looking through Luke's eyes."

Luke is the name of the man who disowned me. I don't honor him with the title of "father" anymore.

"Maybe. But it's a new thing. New things get old fast." People move on. Get bored. Discontented. I don't say that. I don't believe Georgie would ever think like that. But...

Society's a bitch, sometimes.

Georgie's voice is serious and deep, a heavy filet mignon of a voice that makes my thighs clench despite the worried thoughts running around my head. "New things can become old things, favorite things, most precious and cherished things."

In the distance, I spy a glimmer of white. A short, low row of buildings. "I'm sorry I still get like this. Anxious and down on myself." Georgie knows I've dealt with these issues for a long time and that they only got worse after my mother died and my father treated my grief like an excuse to throw off his plans.

"It's fine, my love. It doesn't make you less. It means I get to love you more."

See? I told you he's perfect.

"You know, they say this place has whatever you need. Whatever supernatural occupant stays in the hotel will find the room stocked and prepared to accommodate his needs. I've got an idea. Something that I think will show you just how much I want you—exactly as you are."

Georgie turns into the parking lot. We're the only vehicle. "Let's go see if I'm right."

I CARRY CLAIRE IN MY arms, bridal style. I'd rather carry her with her legs wrapped around me and her pussy stretched around my cock. For the moment, this will have to do. I swipe my bank card through the reader at the door and it beeps open. I don't know how much it charged, but I'm not worried. The price will be fair, and the room will be perfect for us thanks to the benevolent fae who maintain this place.

"Whoa." Claire slowly slips from my arms as we cross the threshold. "I... I thought places like this only existed in Vegas."

I look up and around. There are mirrors on the ceiling and on the wall across from the bed. The wall beside the bed has a starburst of silvery mirror designs, showing my surprised face in a dozen little droplets, not fragmented, but crystal clear in each one.

"Oh. This is... overwhelming." Claire bites her lip and clings to my arm.

"For me, it's paradise." I gently guide her to stand in front of me. "Look. I can see your beautiful face a dozen times." I shift and bring her with me, leering at our reflection in the mirror across from the wide, sumptuous bed. "I can see all of you at once."

Claire gives me a slightly uncertain look. "You want that?"

"Yes. Always." I almost say "Duh." (But I'm fairly certain a good husband doesn't say that.) "I've already seen every bit of you before. Intimately." Exploring Claire is my favorite hobby, and she knows it.

"Well, I love exploring you, but you're a hunky Orc."

"And you're a scrumptious siren of a woman. Your point?"

"That I think you're crazy."

"I am—about you." I lead her to the bathroom in the corner of the mirrored room. "Shower and shampoo first. And then..." I rub my hands. "I'm going to explain just how absolutely beautiful you are with plenty of visual aids."

THE SHOWER IS BUILT for two—two dragons that is! Georgie and I fit inside the shower easily. The water is warm and packs plenty of power. Gem-like bottles full of heavenly-scented shampoos and soaps line the wall. Georgie wastes no time selecting one that smells like brown sugar, cinnamon, and vanilla, massaging the shampoo into my scalp and then lathering me all over, paying particular attention to my breasts, thighs, and what's in between. Honestly, it's amazing. It feels like I'm some ancient priestess being adored by her handsome acolyte.

I return the favor, soaping Georgie's chest and sliding a slippery fist over his thick cock, the width of which is easily the size of my wrist—and that doesn't include the thick bulge at the base, his knot. The soap I chose for him is like honey and spices. "Good enough to eat," I tease, starting to kneel.

"No, no." Georgie grips my shoulders and lowers his head to mine. "Wait. I want you to watch me devouring you. And I want you to see how hot you look when your mouth is full of my cock. The only thing hotter has to be when your pussy is full of my knot."

I whimper. Dirty words in that low, resonant voice send floods of wetness to my already aching center. I want Georgie so bad—but I'm not sure how I feel about seeing my bulges and rolls on display. "I think..."

"I think you should trust me, my love. If you don't like it, we'll stop. Or I'll blindfold you."

Well. I swallow as my pussy gives such a hard pulse that I'm surprised there isn't a noise emanating from it. "That's an idea," I squeak.

THE FAE ARE CLEVER little things. Kind, too, in this case. I noticed it right away when I looked long enough at the mirror by the bed. I looked good—better than good. Flawless. I looked like a green Fabio, back in his prime. Taller. Thicker. More muscular.

It clicked while we were in the shower. These mirrors are more than plentiful. They're enchanted. They don't show a person as perfect—I still had burn scars, dimples, and divots—but they didn't seem to matter. These mirrors don't show you as you see yourself. They show you accurately—but better.

I think I was seeing myself through Claire's eyes.

It takes humans a little longer to see magic sometimes, especially if it isn't something they grew up with. I can't wait for Claire to see herself the way I see her. I hope one day she realizes how utterly breathtaking she is, but in the meantime, I'm happy to lend her my eyes.

GEORGIE AND I TUMBLE to the bed, mouths mating and hands sliding. "On your back, *wife*," he whispers, and I'm putty. I flop back, trying to avoid looking in the mirrors—but they're everywhere.

I'll just look at Georgie instead, at how perfect he looks, with that satiny smooth back that has the texture of supple leather, how his hair looks when it's damp, all blondes and browns spreading over his shoulders.

Hey. I look pretty good, too. Do my boobs really look like that?

In the mirror, they fall to the side, but they look... Well, if I had to use a word, I would say *juicy*. Like someone airbrushed me straight out of a pin-up calendar. Not just my top half—all of me, actually. Every inch looks plump and perfect, with skin as smooth as caramel and curves in all the right spots. My stomach is a soft hill, and Georgie wraps one arm over it with a contented groan, his hand possessively squeezing the softness as he smothers his head between my legs and starts to lap away at my pussy.

"You're so perfect," he whispers. "And you taste divine."

I risk a peep at the mirror beyond the bed. After I'm done staring at the glorious green ass and broad shoulders, I crane my neck to see how it looks when Georgie has me on the menu.

As if he can read my mind, Georgie changes positions, sliding from the bed and pulling me to its edge. He kneels at the foot and turns sideways so I can see better as he slides one thick finger into my grasping walls and licks around my clit before sucking it into his mouth.

My breath catches. I know it's me, I know it's not new—but it's so hot to see. I tighten my walls on him and see the spasm in the mirror, feel him fighting to thrust in me—a battle he wins easily.

"You're going to ride me, sweet little doe. Ride me while we both watch. I want to see every inch of my cock slipping into you. Did you have your tea?"

I nod through a moan. Knotting tea is part of my daily routine now. I drink a cup when I wake up and another in the afternoon. It makes human-Orc copulation much easier—especially when it comes to putting something the size of a grapefruit into something the size of a tangerine.

"Good girl."

Georgie praising me as he licks my pussy as I watch? I'm a puddle.

"Mmm, *yummy* girl."

Apparently, a very tasty puddle.

"Your turn," I shimmy away from his mouth, surprised to see that even though I jiggle, it's more of a sensual sway. Georgie's eyes light up as he watches me bounce to my knees. "Up on the bed," I coax. "I'm not the only yummy thing around here." I wrap my fist around his erection and pump my hand over his shaft as my mouth stretches around his head.

IT'S AMAZING HOW MUCH you can revere your wife and mate as the sacred object of your affection—and also watch her suck your cock with sloppy kisses and soft gagging noises as she struggles to swallow more than just the tip. I sweep Claire's hair up into my fist so I can watch her mouthing me, her cheeks bulging, breasts swaying as her hands and mouth work in unison.

She looks like every man's fantasy, with that round ass and the soft fluffy middle, the big breasts that bob as she sucks. I bite my lip and force my eyes to stay open so I can watch this show in fae-sponsored surround-sight.

Claire's eyes are closed one moment then open the next as she looks up at me, cheeks hollowing as she sucks vigorously on my tip, her fist working faster around my thick rod, slippery with my pre-cum and her saliva.

"I don't think I can wait," I hiss.

She pulls back with a wet plop. "You don't have to."

"Don't want to rush and hurt you, not even a little."

"I'm so slippery for you. I don't think that'll happen."

I hope she's right because lust plus a plethora of visual aids are ruining my self-control.

"Come here, sweet stag." Claire climbs astride me, chest to my chest.

"Pretty little doe." I watch in the mirror behind us as Claire positions herself near my cock, but I'm the one who grips my shaft in one hand and her bountiful bottom in the other, squeezing as tight as I like and still feeling like there's acres left to plunder. Claire moans and wraps her arms around my neck, letting me maneuver.

Green nestles into pink, slowly pushing and parting the soft slick folds. Claire whimpers in want when I pause to rub the tip to her clit, watching her opening spasm before I fit myself to her hole and shove in with slow, steady pressure.

I can see her widening around me, stretching over me as her sweet juice drips down my cock. I want to crow with pride at how wet I make her—but she's making me every bit as hard as she is wet. "You're amazing," I whisper, my head just over hers, bent so my lips brush her brow.

In response, Claire wriggles and pushes herself down on me, tight walls straining. I lean back so I can see her stretch. My hips jolt upward without warning when I imagine her stretched over my knot. I bite down softly on her neck, eyes still locked on her mirror image, imagining how she'll look when we're done—gaping open, a river of cream flowing from her. "You are the sexiest thing imaginable. You have no idea what you do to me."

"I can feel it," she whispers, her hand clutching the back of my head, fingers kneading through my hair.

Our bodies start to pump and glide, small movements that turn more and more frenzied. Suddenly, I can't bear that I can't see both her body and her face at the same time.

With a whirl of movement, I lean back and lift Claire up, changing our positions so that she's still sitting on my cock—but now she's facing the mirror.

FACE FLUSHED. BREASTS bouncing. Georgie's arms wrapped over the stomach I used to hate, and his enraptured face pressed close to mine...

Why was I ever afraid to see this moment, this magical thing that happens when my body pulls his so deep inside that we're truly one flesh? I lock my hand around his, gold bands glinting in the light of a dozen reflections.

"Never, ever complain about this masterpiece again," Georgie gently palms one breast before his fingers slide between my legs, circling on my clit. "You're everything good, Claire. Soft. Supple. You were made for a hard world, to make a soft landing for hungry hearts. My prize. My treasure. My bride. Only *I* get to share this body with you."

I nod, too close to coming to speak as Georgie rubs me to the point where I can't hold back. I know once I'm loosened up from an orgasm while his huge cock is in me, it won't be long until his knot works its way in, too.

Georgie grabs me tighter, pulling my back to his chest as his eyes squeeze shut. His face is the real masterpiece, this raw thing of passion and feral beauty. I can't believe he's mine. I can't believe I'm his. "Love you."

"Love you."

The heel of his hand presses just above my mound while the tips of his fingers grind against my clit. Pressure from this huge cock inside means that my body is basically one big orgasm sandwich—and I get to watch what happens.

Georgie's eyes squint. "I want to see how far you squirt when I fuck you like this. When we watch. Do you think you can take my knot tonight, my tight little Claire?"

Georgie is the one who taught me I could squirt—even though it kind of surprised both of us. Now, it's a pretty common occurrence, but it's usually just a hot, wet jet of liquid lust that accompanies my climax. Watching us move together, feeling all the delicious sensations possible, internally, externally, hear his rough, breathless voice in my ear...

"Ffff-uck!" It's a high wail between clenched teeth as my body seems to burst and showers the mirror nearest us with a cascade of clear drops.

While my body is still heaving, Georgie grips my hips and shoves his own up. We rock back until his back hits the bed, then roll until I'm under him. He has all the leverage, all the control, and I love it. I ride the orgasmic high as I feel my body stretching around his knot as he works it into me. There is a burst of pain that dissolves into sparkles of bliss, and another long, rolling wave of orgasm begins.

The best part is that I can turn my head and see it from the side, or look past our bodies and see the erotic image of Georgie knotting me in the mirror behind us. Looking up, I smile at the mirror over the bed. My hair is a sweaty, tangled mess, my skin is pink, and I can't open my eyes all the way.

I look fucking fantastic, a contented sex goddess with her musclebound god mating her. With a sigh, I wrap possessive arms over Georgie's broad torso and dig my fingertips into his beautiful green back. "Mmm. Mine."

"Oh, yes. Always yours." Georgie grins and kisses me. When he stops, he smirks. "Can you see why I can't stop touching you, woman?" He shares a peek into the looking glass with me. "Look at you." He runs a hand over my cheek while his cock pumps deep inside of me.

I moan as I feel his crown jerk and twitch, sending his cum into me, filling me fuller than I once thought possible.

"Look at us," I whisper back, bringing him back to me, fingers netting in his hair. "Together, we're absolutely stunning."

"That's my Claire. Never forget it."

Chapter Six: Deals

Starring the Ghillie Dhu (only in town on rare occasions) and Marina, from various Pine Ridge novels.

"I'm so honored that you could attend, my liege. May I present my bride?"

The Ghillie Dhu smiled at Ardghal Walsh and the beautiful redhead on his arm. "*Sláinte chuig na fir, agus go mairfidh na mná go deo.*" The dark-haired fae nobleman put his hand on the bride's shoulder and bowed to the pooka police officer, the last of a long line of protectors and upholders of the pooka's nobler nature. "Be fruitful."

The couple blushed and looked startled, but the Ghillie Dhu didn't mind. He meant his blessing to be taken seriously, shocking or not. Pookas were a dying race. That was one reason he'd invited himself to the wedding. That, and he hadn't been to the little paranormal-friendly town of Pine Ridge in many years. To be truthful, he rarely interacted with anyone, fae or human, these days. He preferred to appear only to lost children and hikers in need of help.

Being immortal was lonely. This wedding, filled with humans and supernatural beings alike, drove home just how hungry he was for companionship.

The lights dimmed. The bride and groom began a slow, romantic dance that made his chest ache. Couples around the room were leaning against one another, stealing kisses, and exchanging glances.

Even though the wedding dance was graceful and chaste, there was an underlying current of sensuality between the bride and groom. Every motion spoke of longing.

He was very familiar with longing.

Gill, as he preferred to be called by his friends (the few he had), slipped out of the reception and began the several-mile walk back to the little motel he was staying at.

WALKING IN THE CHILLY October night was nothing for a woodland fae like himself. And stamina was no issue for Gill. "I could walk five hundred miles, and I could walk five hundred more—and I would still feel restless." The restlessness settled between his thighs as he walked along the silvery ribbon of the river that ran through Pine Ridge and into the spacious plot of land that surrounded a small, ordinary-looking motel—Country Pines.

But just like Gill, who appeared as a short, raven-haired man with sharp, clever features and a lithe, willowy frame, the motel had a secret. The place was maintained by benevolent fae and only appeared to those who were able to see or sense paranormal beings. The rooms were constantly changing to meet the needs of their occupants.

Gill knew he would be given a warm welcome in the home of most Pine Ridge residents (well, the non-human residents), but he didn't want to spend a night and the next morning making awkward small talk or being treated like royalty—even though he *was* a fae noble, his rank never ascertained since he the only one of his kind and court.

He kicked a pebble in the river, feeling morose and out of sorts. "All right, kinsmen." He swished his long, pine-green cloak around him and pushed back the hood to stare at the motel up the hill. "Let's see if you can truly give this weary traveler what he needs."

"Are you talking to the hotel or the river?"

Gill whirled and smothered a cry of surprise. The most ravishing, pale temptress he'd ever seen was standing in the water, holding a stone in her hand.

"You dropped this," she smirked, revealing a tiny sliver of sharp-pointed teeth.

"Are you a selkie?" Gill was startled into asking.

"No! Rusalka. What are you?"

"I am the Ghillie Dhu, lord of mountains and forests, protector of innocent souls."

"Oh. Cool." The creature smiled at him, nostrils twitching once, like a curious bunny.

"And you?"

"Rusalka. Thief of souls, drainer of lifeforce, scourge of lustful men."

Gill drew back, startled.

"Reformed!" She waved a careless hand. "What brings you to town? Looking to settle in where it's safe to be a monster?"

Gill smiled at her. "It's tempting, but no. I have a place to protect, and my sentinels will only keep travelers and innocents safe for so long." He looked out over the dark shapes of pines and mountains as if seeing far across the water, watching through the eyes of the owls and stags he had told to lead the endangered to safety in his place.

"Just passing through? Looking for company?"

Gill gave the watery woman a startled look. "How did you know?"

"About the company?" She smiled, sharp teeth on display beneath wet ruby-red lips. "I came here looking for the same thing. When I'm really desperate, I come to this place."

Courtliness was in his blood—or what passed for it. With a bow, Gill extended his hand and offered to help the rusalka ashore. "Desperate for what? Company?"

"Of a particular kind." On land, she stood a few inches taller than him, her bountiful breasts much closer to his face than he would have imagined—and much more visible than was appropriate thanks to her translucent, water-logged dress.

"What kind?"

"The kind that feeds my needs to consume—without taking a life. Just a little bit of his life force, what a man gives a woman naturally when he pours himself into her." Her hand dared to rest on the deep green velvet of his cloak. "Mm. A well-dressed hero comes to my aid. We love a short king. Care to give me a little help this evening, Your Highness?"

He smiled up at her, amusement on his features. "Don't you know not to make bargains with the fae?"

"Don't you know not to make deals with demons?" she whispered with a wink, fingers raking through his hair as she pushed herself a little closer.

He could feel her wetness rubbing off on his chest. "Do you ever get dry?" he asked.

"Not in the place where it counts."

The restless ache in his middle turned pointed. "What would your deal consist of?"

"You and I keep each other busy tonight. You get your company. I get one hell of a fancy dinner," she smiled, the width of her grin almost unsettling, "and we part company in the morning. You have to go back to your protectorate, and I don't think I can live off of fairy food. Your souls are just a little hard to digest."

Gill paused, looking into eyes that shone deep ocean blue—yet had a wavering flame in the center, a roving dot of red. "What's your name?"

"Ah. Doesn't that mean you'll have power over me?"

With a sudden twist, Gill wound his hand into the long mane of dark, dripping hair, making her gasp. He brought her down for a kiss, his knee sliding firmly between her plump, shapely thighs. Gill couldn't stop the moan from escaping his lips. If ever there was a woman designed to tempt a man, it was this one. He pushed her back as he felt her go limp in his arms, sagging into his touch with a hungry cry. "There! You're already in my power—and you like it that way. We'll exchange strengths for the evening. Name?"

"Marina."

He could hear just the faintest trace of an accent when she spoke. "Call me Gill."

"DO YOU NEED TO STAY in the water?" Gill asked.

"Not every moment. However, if you want to see some aquatic acrobatics, I'm sure you'd survive a dip in the river."

Gill considered. "Bed," he decided. "And on the way, explain how it works—this appetite of yours."

Marina followed him up the hill to his room at Country Pines. "Sexual energy is like... well, like a stem cell for lifeforce. Without sex, there's no reproduction. Men give one of the key ingredients for life when they make love. If I take a soul, I'll be much more powerful and much fuller for longer. If I let a man expend his energy with me—and feed me his essence, I can survive. I just need to feed far more often."

"You're like a succubus?"

"They get all the credit," Marina gave a bitter smile. "My needs are just a little bit greater. I need..." her lips stilled and her hand made its way to his arm, then his thigh, and then between them, "I need your cum. Might as well skip the hints and tell you straight out."

Gill paused. "What about pregnancy?"

Marina's face clouded. "Only Koshchei can impregnate us—and he does."

"I'm not familiar with that name."

"The patriarch demon of the rusalka. He lives and dies and is reborn from the souls we harvest for him. When he's reborn, he picks several handmaids to... refill the stock."

Gill blinked. "That sounds very complex—and also rather like inbreeding."

"If I were made of human blood and DNA, I would worry. But I'm not, and I can't get pregnant. The Koshchei won't choose me to 'honor' with his seed because I don't send him gifts of souls. If he chooses me out of spite—well, I know one loophole, but I really hope I don't have to use it." She shuddered and followed Gill into the warm hotel room.

"Oooh. Stylish." Gill took a moment to appreciate the room's simple, rustic beauty. It reminded him very much of his own home, all dark woods, greens, grays, and reds. He didn't admire it for long, turning to his companion. "It sounds as though your existence could be very tenuous, held in the grip of an elder demon you no longer wish to serve. If you ever need help—"

Marina interrupted him with a kiss. "No, no. I have help here. Pine Ridge is full of some of the strongest magic in the world and the kindest people. If Koshchei comes to me, I have people to assist me, places to hide. With any luck, he'll be asleep for a century yet. Tonight, I don't want to worry about anything but making my new friend feel welcome."

His eyes slowly traveled down her clinging white dress. Wide hips, narrow waist, breasts that were round and buoyant with dark pink nipples. "Isn't that dress a little revealing?"

"That's the point," Marina laughed. "I *enjoy* revealing this body to men. The ones who aren't in love look with their eyes—and they like what they see." Her hand peeled down one wet sleeve, then the other, exposing her dead white shoulders and the swell of her breasts. "Would you like me to demonstrate just how comfortable I am in this body—and how comfortable I'd like to be with yours?"

Gill nodded, swallowing a lustful little cry. He didn't speak much as a rule, and now he was afraid of saying too much. There hadn't been a woman in his life in a long, long time—and he had a feeling there were very few women in the world like Marina.

MARINA LOVED THIS PART. The way men look at her with lust. Gill shed his cloak and revealed a compact yet rangy body, a form that looked as if it had spent years crouching in thickets and scaling rocks. Dark curly hair, dark eyes with flecks of gold, and a permanently sun-kissed complexion from being a literal ruler of the forests and mountains.

But when he looked at her, she, some little soul-sucking demon from the icy seas at the top of the world, was his queen. All he wanted.

Marina might play at being vulnerable, but as soon as she locked eyes with her night's delicacy, she was the predator. It all came by making them think she was making herself weak—while in reality, she was just baiting the perfect hook.

Her dress slid to the floor in a long, flowing puddle, revealing skin as white as permafrost—except for the dark pink of her nipples and the perfect ruddy brown of the curls between her thighs, kept in the latest style of a perfect triangular patch.

She swished and swayed, walking closer to him—then she turned and walked to the glowing fire that smelled like wet wood and peat smoke. "Pass me that comforter?"

"Duvet." Gille handed her the thick, quilted blanket from the top of his bed.

"Men say I'm a little bit chilly at first. This will warm us both up." Marina spread the blanket in front of the fire and reclined on it, one hand fondling her honeydew-sized breasts, thumbing the hard nipple. The other slid between her thighs, splitting her slit apart.

Gill let out a shuddering breath. "Shouldn't I do that for you?" he asked, slowly unbuttoning the white shirt he'd worn to the wedding.

"You can, but I like to make sure I'm just right for you."

"Isn't that your lover's job?" he asked.

Marina hesitated. She didn't take lovers, not exactly. She had sexual partners. Most of them were curious college boys who came quickly and worked her body with energy and a total lack of finesse. "No. I don't need him to do that."

"What if he wants to do that? I could have any number of lovers, rusalka. I didn't ask my kinsmen to deliver a quick fuck. I asked for companionship—even if it's only for one night."

Marina swallowed when Gill slid his trousers down revealing the perfect end to the muscular torso and the rippling thighs—a sturdy, thick erection already suffused with blood that made it look deep pink. "The perfect sweet to suck on," she purred.

"Is that so? What about those razors you call teeth, my lady?"

Marina giggled. My lady. Ha. Like she was anything remotely resembling refined. "I suck, not bite. Trust me." She patted the floor beside her head, rolling to one side. She ran a hand over her hip as Gill knelt next to her.

"Shouldn't I know something about you first? Don't we talk? Have a drink?"

Marina looked up at him and ran her long, pointed tongue over her lips and then jutted her head forward to catch the sweet bridge of muscle that made up Gill's inner thigh. "Okay. We'll talk. Tell me your favorite drink."

"Whiskey, neat."

"Vodka, nearly freezing."

Gill closed his eyes and leaned further in, tight buttocks clenching as he risked trusting her.

"Another thing you might like to know about me—I never disappoint." Marina curled her tongue gently over his shaft and sucked him slowly into her mouth, guarding him with her tongue and cheeks, keeping him in a cone of soft, wet muscle.

Gill's hands flexed and then one tangled into her hair. The other hand delved between her legs, mimicking the actions of her own fingers, his touch insistent. "And I'm quite flexible."

Marina gasped as his fingers danced on her clit and then pushed down, deeper, opening her up. His fingers were warm and slightly rough, the sort of hands that belonged to a man who climbs through woods and mountains all day. But they were incredibly confident and thorough, sweeping in slow arcs inside of her, bringing her wetness to cover his fingers until each thrust of his hand made her sound obscenely wet.

But fair is fair, Marina thought as Gill relaxed and started to fuck her mouth in time with his searching fingers. Each movement of his hips earned a noisy wet gulp from her mouth.

"What else would you like to know?" Gill asked, his cock deep in her mouth, looking down on her with an amused smile.

Marina dared to let her sharp teeth tease the hot skin of his shaft. He pulled out with wide eyes. "I have manners. I won't talk with my mouth full. Usually."

"Given those pretty daggers you carry, my dear, I don't blame you."

"Pretty?" Marina purred. She knew she was sexually desirable—and she knew most humans never noticed the inhuman details of her form, like the sharp teeth, the too-wide mouth, and the nearly permanent cool wetness of her skin.

But Gill could see her exactly as she was.

"Oh, yes. Incredibly beautiful. Dangerously so."

"Danger is something you must be familiar with," Marina whispered. "You know how the deep woods and the high hills can be."

"Mm. Indeed, I do. It's a clever lass who can spot the fact that this wee man knows as much about danger as some of your bigger, fiercer beasties."

Marina arched her back to slip his fingers deeper inside of her, lips parting in surprise at how good it felt and how skilled his fingers were as they smoothly zeroed in on the sensitive pieces of her demonic anatomy. She was built differently than human women, with her erogenous zones being broader and more plentiful. It meant sex was almost guaranteed to be enjoyable—but Gill was ensuring it would be more than just "pleasant."

"You don't have to tell me what else you like, pet. I can tell you like what I'm doing by how your cunny grips my fingers. You'd like to swallow the lot, wouldn't you?"

Marina moaned as he added a third finger to her slippery opening, thrusting his hand in time with his hips. All she could do was moan.

"That's a very pretty sound," he crooned, his free hand tangling in her hair, pressing his cock deeper into her mouth, touching the edges of her throat.

She upped the suction, stroking him with her curling, flexible tongue, pumping his cock while her cheeks hollowed around him. By his sudden uneven breathing and the way his fingers simply rested in her for a moment, she could tell that Gill was close to giving her what she wanted.

Rusalka skills. We win every time.

"Oh. Ohh!" Gill breathed in hard through his nose, eyes closing, compact body tensing as Marina gave him the equivalent of a hand-job and oral stimulation at once.

She would have to gloat later. Her mouth was otherwise engaged, milking the sweet drops of his pre-cum into her mouth. If some women complained they didn't like the taste, Marina had never minded. The essence of men was her favorite sustenance, and each had a delicately different flavor, like different vintages of wine.

Gill was pure whiskey, finely aged until it was smooth and smoky. And if only she could get him to unstopper this particular decanter, then she was sure she could drink her fill. With a throaty sound that was marred by the jerky rhythm of his hips, growing ever more erratic at her urging, Marina reached one milky white hand up and dragged her crimson nails down over his chest and belly, leaving lovely little red lines before swirling over his thigh and slipping a finger between them to dance over his tightening sack.

Come for me, she thought, hoping he could hear her thoughts. She looked up at his face, currently tense with his eyes screwed up tight. Her nails dug into one buttock and she dared let her teeth graze his shaft.

Gill grunted, glared down, and met her burning eyes.

Marina knew she was throwing her most hypnotic gaze—but she doubted it would work on a fae, especially if he were disinclined to be lured.

But the fae royal she'd snagged for the evening gave every indication of enjoying her temptation. "I'll return the favor, demoness. Promise."

With a shudder, Gill gripped the back of her head, hips stopped in mid-pump, unleashing in her mouth with sharp, strangled breaths.

Marina sighed, warmth flooding through her system instantly as she drank him in, letting her tongue loosen its stroking grasp. She licked the tip gently, sucking on him as he slowed, working out every last drop of his cum.

"Mm. Yummy." Marina licked her lips and smiled at Gill as he sank onto the blanket beside her.

"My God, woman."

Marina smiled up at him. She rather liked all the names Gill called her—my lady, lass, demoness, even the simple term of "woman." "Good?"

"Extraordinary." Gill's eyes were glazed as he stared at her, then the fire, seeming dazed. "It's been a long time since I've been with anything close to an equal. And that was just your mouth."

Marina tossed her hair over her shoulder. It was losing its damp, heavy look and turning into chestnut waves as it dried, the fire giving it a warmer glow that would go nicely with the dancing flame in the center of her pupils. "Well. I do practice. A lot."

Gill laughed. "I'm glad to be on the receiving end of the skills. Now, I, on the other hand, am probably rusty. But let's see what I can do to make you happy."

Marina ran a finger over her lips, seeking any stray drops. "Oh, you'll find I'm very responsive."

Gill leaned on one elbow, scooting up so his head was just above hers as he reclined on his hip. "Then that means I have to do a very good job, doesn't it? Otherwise, you might think I took advantage of your natural gifts and dinnae prove m'self as I should." Gill ran his fingers through her hair, smiling slightly.

"Your accent comes out more when you're flirting."

"Ah, well. Let's see what happens to your voice when it's screaming for me."

GILL SMILED AS HE LOWERED his head over one perfect sphere of a breast. He sucked her nipple into his mouth as his fingers started rubbing and stroking between Marina's legs, finding her warm, wet, and welcoming. She was incredibly responsive, just as she'd said, but that didn't mean he would take the lazy option and only think of his own enjoyment.

"What do the men you usually dine on do for you, love?"

"It's more like what do I do for them. I don't care, as long as they come inside of me. Any opening will do. I'm absorbing the essence of his being, not worrying about calories, after all. But most don't do what you're doing." She ended her little speech with a cry, head lolling back and hips widening. "I need you in me. I can feel you're ready for another round."

Gill smirked. He was, but there was more to explore before giving her what she wanted most. "Do they lick your pretty little cunny? It is such a pretty one. Perfect pinks and creams. You're just made to look like a sweetshop window, aren't you?"

"More like the window of the naughty novelty store," Marina corrected with a giggle as he switched breasts, taking the other hard, crinkled nipple into his mouth.

Gill rolled on top of her, body following mouth, enjoying feeling her soft, supple curves under him, tempted beyond words to push his stiff cock into her sweet wetness. Instead, he rocked his belly to hers, letting his cock rub against her clit, feeling her strain and grind, aching to trap him between her thighs.

Instead, he slid like a breeze through the branches of a bare tree, coasting down her warm, buttery skin until his head was between her thighs. "Open."

No blushing modesty here. The rusalka thrust her legs apart, pussy up and glistening like a rose after the rain. Gill planted a kiss on her petals, nose burying in her skin and the curls atop it. Naturally, she smells delicious, Gill thought. *She has every other attraction a predator can have to bring its prey into its trap. Poor thing. Always letting herself be the prey, just to survive without harming others. I'm glad Pine Ridge offers her a safe haven. Wish I could offer her something else for the night.*

His tongue swirled over her, slow and lazy, taking his time to savor her taste, something like brandied peaches—a favorite dessert of his. He wondered if she tasted different to each man, based on his preferences.

"Pretty pearl," he murmured, nuzzling his lips down to capture the perfect round bubble of pink that was her clit. He wasted no time before lapping around the tiny crown and then sucking the entire thing into his mouth, tongue stroking and flicking the way hers had.

"Ohhh. Oh, fuck." Marina's fingertips clutched his hair, first one hand, then two.

"In time." He resumed sucking, adding his three thrusting fingers to the mix, feeling her hips try to escape his grasp, feeling her strong hands try to drag him up. He pinched her full, round bottom hard and kept his thumb and forefinger there, pinning her with just a gesture. "Good girl. Let someone else do the work."

"I just want you," Marina whimpered, voice much smaller and more timid than earlier.

It cut him unexpectedly deep, especially knowing what kind of life she had, what kind of "punishment" she could expect simply for refusing to harm humans. "You could return to Scotland with me, Marina. I wouldn't expect you to stay by my side, but the places where I roam are under my protection. I would hate to see someone like you harmed by someone like this vengeful soul-collector you mentioned."

This time, when she tugged him up, he came willingly, settling his hand between their bodies so that he could watch her come on his fingers as she thrashed her beautiful head in the light of the flickering flames.

Her last gasping cry was his name—before his kiss stole it from her lips. "Pretty Marina."

"Sweet Gill. Generous Gill. You know… You are the first man who has ever offered to take me away—to try to protect me."

"I wouldn't expect you to be some sort of… mistress. I would expect you to swim in my rivers—and play nice with the kelpies and selkies, mind."

Marina kissed him again, guiding her hand to his cock, rubbing him with slow, hypnotic strokes that made him ache to thrust into her. He bucked into her hand and found himself sinking into a pink paradise instead.

The rusalka's womanhood wasn't like anything he'd felt before. His fingers hadn't fully conveyed how wonderful it would be to be inside of her, but her insides were incredibly soft and silky. Despite their smoothness, her walls were covered in delicate textures that massaged every inch of him.

"How many men are in your part of the world? How many unattached men who would let me feed on them—and feed their desires?"

"Ah. I prefer the out of the way places, lass. Rarely see a hiker or hunter."

"And I can't live like that. And your cold waters of the North Sea send me closer than ever to where Koshchei will awaken. No. I'll stay here. I have friends here." She laid a hand against his bronzed cheek. "And now I have a friend somewhere else."

Gill smiled as he rocked into her, intensity building faster than he wanted. "Your accent does come out a bit more when you're about to come, pretty thing."

Marina only smiled. "Don't hold back. Let me have you as many times as I can in one night, yes?"

It was tempting. Was that giving in?

"I can go all night. I have untapped reserves."

Marina's eyes lit up. "Mm. So can I. And—well into the next day when I'm properly fed." Her nails ran over his back and down the cleft of his ass, teasing his rim as he thrust in hard, his balls slapping into her juicy pussy.

Gill let himself fall into her trap, knowing it wasn't much of a trap at all. He hammered into her hard and fast, listening to her breathless laughter turn into a keening cry as he pounded into her.

"Give me all of you," he urged, pushing her legs back.

Marina held them to her chest, nodding and whimpering as she rubbed her clit and let him have every last inch of her.

His hands moved from the floor to her breasts, leaning on her as he gripped them hard, squashing the softness between his fingers as she screamed his name and begged him.

"Come in me! I want to feel you let go again, deep inside this time." Marina's words switched between English and something ancient, something he couldn't understand with his ears, but he felt in his heart. Desperation and hunger. Loneliness. Longing.

The flames in her gaze blazed in him and he doubled his speed, feeling less human and more wild in her presence, a thing of rushing water rising to meet this river demon with fire in her eyes.

He didn't love the rusalka, but he suddenly felt as though he knew her well, on a deep, craveable level. Gill's mouth descended on hers, stoppering her cries. Her deadly teeth slid through the edge of his lower lip, dotting the moment of his release with a hint of pain.

Like meeting Marina. Beautiful. Sensual. Just a little bit painful.

His seed pulsed out into her in long jets and he felt her muscles drawing it in, sucking him and his essence in deep.

Like she never wants to let me go.

Like she never wants to let any of us go.

And maybe this is how men drown in her, giving her everything, letting their souls fly into her pools and her furnaces.

As Gill felt the world drifting farther away, Marina suddenly gasped and broke their kiss, shaking her head and smiling softly. "Thank you, my darling new friend," she whispered. "Don't fall too deeply, forest king. Stay in my shallows, and I'll always welcome you back."

Gill knew they would make love again, maybe a dozen times over the night or the course of a few days, and then they'd be done—maybe forever.

He didn't want to reject her lovely offer to return, but at the same time—he wished for something better for her. "Welcome me back as often as you like, lover. But I hope you find the one who contents ye, keeps you warm and full, and treats you like the queen you are."

Marina blinked up at him.

Funny how her tears don't put out the flames, Gill thought, brushing her hair back from her sweating temples.

"No wonder you're a legend," she whispered, leg lazily draping over his calf to keep him inside her even as he softened.

He wasn't soft for long, those magical muscles of hers already stroking and squeezing him back to life."Ah, pet. It takes one to know one."

About the Author

Bestselling and award-winning author S.C. Principale believes in writing stories she wants to read, which is why she writes steamy characters who need happy endings (and she always delivers on the HEA). S.C. lives in historic Chester County, Pennsylvania, where haunted battlegrounds serve as never-ending inspiration. S.C. is a self-proclaimed history nerd, following old mysteries, baking, and leading theater and musical groups. Her home life consists of scrounging space for her laptop without tripping over two kids, two dogs, a mischievous chinchilla, and the most patient, sexy husband in the world. **Join her mailing list for a free gift!**[1] Or join her **Patreon**[2] for exclusive scenes, bonus content, NSFW art of your favorite couples, and so much more.

scprincipaleauthor@gmail.com

Author Website and Newsletter [3]
Patreon [4]
Twitter [5]
Instagram [6]

---

1. https://bookhip.com/HWDVHHH
2. https://www.patreon.com/scprincipale
3. https://scprincipale.wixsite.com/website
4. https://www.patreon.com/scprincipale
5. https://twitter.com/SCPrincipale

[Facebook](#)[7]
[S.C.'s Sultry Sweethearts Facebook Readers Group](#)[8]
[Monster Brides Monster Fans](#)[9]
[Tiktok](#)[10]
[Goodreads](#)[11]
[Amazon](#) [12]

---

6. https://www.instagram.com/s.c.principale/

7. https://www.facebook.com/WritesandBites

8. https://www.facebook.com/groups/668289727695362

9. https://www.facebook.com/groups/764631992003020

10. https://www.tiktok.com/@scprincipaleauthor

11. https://www.goodreads.com/author/show/14847508.S_C_Principale

12. https://www.amazon.com/S.C.-Principale/e/B01FZZL28I%3Fref=dbs_a_mng_rwt_sc-ns_share

Also By S.C. Principale

Paranormal Romance
Pine Ridge Universe
Pale Girl[1]
Mountain Bound: A Monstrous Love Story[2]
Vampire in Vegas: The Complete Trilogy[3]
The Minotaur's Valentine[4]
Pumpkin Spice and Speed Dating[5]
My Name on Your Lips[6]
All I Never Wished For[7]
The Orc's Christmas Romance[8]
Haunted Hearts: A Monster Brides Romance[9]
Nothing to Hyde: A Monster Brides Romance[10]
Velvet Wings[11]
The Pine Loft Culinary Collection[12]

---

1. http://books2read.com/u/bPQ0aJ

2. http://books2read.com/u/bPQp6A

3. http://books2read.com/u/3RLqXY

4. https://books2read.com/minotaursvalentine

5. https://books2read.com/pumpkinspiceandspeeddating

6. https://books2read.com/mynameonyourlips

7. https://books2read.com/allIneverwishedfor

8. https://books2read.com/orcschristmasromance

9. https://books2read.com/hauntedheartsmb

10. https://books2read.com/nothingtohyde

11. https://books2read.com/velvetwings

[Dirty December](#)[13]
[Love at Country Pines](#)[14]
[Stone-Cold Groom: A Monster Brides Romance](#)[15]
B-Deviled: A Monster Brides Romance

Felix Orbus Series
[Possessed by the Leonid King](#)[16]
[Taken by the Tigerite](#)[17]
[Lynxian in Love](#)[18]
[Loved by the Leopardine](#)[19]
Saved by the Servali

Forgotten Gods Series
[Forgotten Gods: Volume One](#)[20]
[Forgotten Gods: Volume Two](#)[21]
[Saving Medusa](#)[22]

---

12. https://books2read.com/pineloftculinarycollection

13. https://books2read.com/dirtydecember

14. https://books2read.com/loveatcountrypines

15. https://books2read.com/stonecoldgroom

16. https://books2read.com/leonidking

17. https://books2read.com/takenbythetigerite

18. https://books2read.com/lynxianinlove

19. https://books2read.com/lovedbytheleopardine

20. https://books2read.com/forgottengodsvolumeone

21. https://www.amazon.com/kindle-vella/story/B0BSDMBHMC

22. https://www.amazon.com/kindle-vella/story/B0C9SGXR7D

CrossRealms Universe
[CrossRealms: You an' Me Against the World](http://books2read.com/u/bwKrvP)
[CrossRealms: Healing Hope](http://books2read.com/u/4ApQoK)
[CrossRealms: Gestures](https://books2read.com/u/mlAJJA)
[CrossRealms: A Helpful Gentleman](https://books2read.com/u/3kPnER)
[CrossRealms: Wicked Woods](http://books2read.com/u/m0B8GA)
[CrossRealms: Shattered](https://books2read.com/u/mBwEev)
[CrossRealms: Mended](https://books2read.com/u/baDAPa)
[CrossRealms: Whole](https://books2read.com/u/mKpo9d)

Romantic Suspense
[Madeline](http://books2read.com/u/mg18BR)
[Passion](http://books2read.com/u/3n5DX6)
[Deep Cover](https://books2read.com/deepcover)
[Risky Business in Rovigo](https://books2read.com/riskybusinessinrovigo)

Contemporary Romance

<u>Turning theTables</u>[35]
<u>Repairs</u>[36]
<u>Chocolate Kisses</u>[37]
<u>Chocolate Krinkles and Two Kris Kringles</u>[38]
<u>Books and Suits: A Friends-to-Lovers Romance</u>[39]
<u>Belgravia Security</u>[40]
<u>The Man with the Umbrella</u>[41]
<u>Off-Court</u>[42]
<u>Risky Business in Rovigo</u>[43]

Historical Romance
<u>Alliance</u>[44]

---

35. http://books2read.com/u/mv1R18

36. http://books2read.com/u/br1oVZ

37. http://books2read.com/u/mg1oYz

38. http://books2read.com/u/mVRwkJ

39. http://books2read.com/u/49LMB0

40. https://www.amazon.com/kindle-vella/story/B09DDHWF3C

41. https://books2read.com/themanwiththeumbrella

42. https://books2read.com/offcourt

43. https://books2read.com/riskybusinessinrovigo

44. https://www.amazon.com/kindle-vella/story/B0B4F2RB94

The Minotaur's Valentine

By S.C. Principale

Milo has finally met the girl of his dreams. She's funny, into 80's metal, loves animals, and wants to be a vet.

And that might come in handy since he's half-bull—a minotaur, to be exact.

But Libby is 100% human and not even aware of the monsters and magic that exist in her new town of Pine Ridge, New York. Everyone tells Milo to be patient and stay in the shadows. Libby's smart and she'll eventually figure out that something's different about this innocent-looking suburb...

Libby Ingersol loves Pine Ridge, but it's lonely being the new girl in town. As another Valentine's Day looms, single Libby is desperate to get out and mingle. When she tries the Pine Ridge club scene, things go wildly wrong.

Can a shy minotaur who wears his heart on his hoof make things go right and salvage Libby's Valentine's night?

The Minotaur's Valentine is a feel-good monster romance with a cinnamon roll hero. Just a warning... cinnamon isn't the only spice you'll find in this happily-ever-after tale of monster love!

---

1. https://books2read.com/b/minotaursvalentine

Chapter One: Milo

The Night Market is exactly what it says it is. It's a market that's only open at night. It looks like one of those flea markets or farmers' markets that are set up in the civic center parking lot or a school gym during winter break. In the case of the Pine Ridge Night Market, there are about two dozen small stalls set up in the empty lot behind the Pine Loft Coffee Shop. We sell everything from homemade candy and potpourri to weapons for the discerning demon hunter and pre-made potions for nervous spellcasters.

Obviously, you have to know where to look. (And when to look. We're not open every night.)

And humans... humans aren't excluded, especially not humans who've lived in Pine Ridge for a long time, but most won't see the Night Market the way I do.

I don't have specially enhanced vision or anything. No superpowers. I'm just your average, twenty-something minotaur. I put on my jeans one hoof at a time, just like everyone else.

"Milo. Can you fix my watch fob?"

"What's the trouble, Mr. Minegold? Ooh, hey, J.J." I take the watch from the tall, thin, distinguished man wrapped in a black frock coat and bright tartan muffler. His adopted grandson, J.J., is strapped to his hip in one of those stretchy baby-sling contraptions. I look around for something to give the kid, something that won't kill him. I reach under the stall into my big red tackle box and take out several inches of silver chain. "Here you go, little man. Oh!" I draw back at the last second. "It's silver. Can he touch it?"

"Silver doesn't harm Jesse Jakob." Mr. Minegold savors the name, letting his accent become more pronounced as he caresses the curly little head. "Jesse Jakob, you naughty mite! You have tossed off your wooly hat. Your mama and papa won't like that. I must retrace my steps, Milo. I confess I was lingering too long at the fudge stand!"

"I can understand that, Mr. Minegold! I'll look at the watch fob, and you find J.J.'s hat." I wave them off. J.J. waggles his chubby fist, which is now curled around the silver chain.

Dang. Kids are cute. Even human kids. I know J.J. isn't fully human, but he looks human. His dad, Jesse, is a vamp (so is Mr. Minegold), and his mom is... something demon-y? I don't know the details, but she is gorgeous.

My brother, Bill, would tease me if he were still living in town. He'd call me out on my interest in interspecies couples. As soon as Bill turned twenty, he moved back to the family homestead in Greece. He has a beautiful wife and two kids now. He'd also tell me that I'm running out of time to find a girl. I'm almost thirty. Minotaur women like their bulls young, that's what he'd say.

But I don't want to marry a person based on their outer shell, that's what I'd tell him.

And that's how the fight would start. That's how the same dumb argument always starts. And every time, my parents snort and exchange glances and go take their coffee into the kitchen.

I force my focus back to Minegold's watch. I press the fob on the thick, brassy case, careful to keep it pointing at the floor.

Plink.

A thin wooden stake clatters to the cement. It was only a quarter of an inch wide, tipped in silver, and reinforced with an iron core. It *should* have shot out with the force of a small, lightweight missile. "Ahh. The spring action is gone," I mutter, retrieving the stake from where it had landed between my hooves. It was supposed to spring out with a pretty hefty punch so that its razor-sharp tip and inner core (fully encased in wood) would penetrate deep enough to take out a vampire or a werewolf at close range.

Of course, I'm not advocating the killing of *all* vampires and werewolves. The established supernatural community of Pine Ridge is mostly peaceful and dedicated to keeping evil-doers out of our fair little city.

Mr. Minegold, who has been here since the end of World War II, organized a neighborhood patrol long, long ago to drive out or exterminate undesirables. My grandfather came over around the same time as Minegold. But since minotaurs in rural New York have a little trouble blending in, my family has always hung out in the shadows, worked nights, and made friends with other night-dwelling creatures, like Mr. Minegold. He can get around okay in the daytime as long as it's cloudy, but he prefers the night and stays inside during the day whenever he can.

Minotaurs protect. We guarded King Minos' wife and children against his insane rage by taking them into the labyrinth and pledging we would die before they were harmed. Greek history can say what it wants, but minotaurs have always been friends to the weakest among us. In the modern age, that usually means we make the firepower to hunt the *real* monsters.

I slip my headphones (the wireless kind so they don't get tangled around my horns) over my head and cue up Metallica on my phone. "Hey! Mr. Minegold?" I shout down the row of market stalls.

"Yes, Milo?" He turns at once. Vampires have amazing hearing.

"You need a new spring! Twenty bucks and twenty minutes?"

Mr. Minegold beams and waves back, earning smiles and curious looks from the people pushing past him. "You are a godsend! See you in twenty minutes!" He jiggles J.J. on his hip, unearthing a blue knitted cap with a fluffy white pom pom and ear flaps. "Ah! J.J.! There's your hat! Did you have it stuffed in my pocket this whole time? You clever little dumpling!"

My God. Kids are adorable…

I turn up the volume.

Chapter Two: Libby

Have you ever had coffee so good you want to take it back to bed with you? Maybe whisper in its ear and coo a few sweet nothings?

Why, yes. I am single, thank you.

But, that perfectly describes the cinnamon streusel coffee from The Pine Loft Coffee Shop. It was delicious and decadent, sweet and full of warm spices. And cheap. Criminally cheap.

Everything in my new town is ultra affordable. My godmother says that I should consider it a red flag.

"There's nothing cheap about New York, Libby!" Aunt Karen had lectured a few months ago, her thin arms crossed over her bony chest, staring at me with her wild, not-all-there eyes before turning back to her blaring television.

My godmother is a lot like a feral cat, whereas me, I'm a stray. She didn't want to take me in, and I didn't want to stay with her. When she and my mother were best friends back in high school, "Aunt Karen" became my godmother. Then my mom went to work at a daycare where I could come for free, and Aunt Karen moved in with a way-older guy, discovered daytime television, and developed a taste for flavored vodkas. By the time my mom passed away when I was eighteen, Aunt Karen was all alone. Rich, lecherous "Uncle Amir" had been done in by a spectacular cardiac arrest in a strip joint while choking on a cigar and trying to get change from a five out of a neon bikini.

I didn't want to live with Aunt Karen, even sans the not-so-dearly-departed Uncle Amir, so I was a stray. On my own, surviving on scraps of part-time jobs, and a few months of my mother's Social Security benefits before they cut me off.

I went to a cheap college and lived on campus. Antonia College isn't the jewel of the state education system, so they offer perks for coming back each semester, and bonuses when you take summer classes. I had no complaints. I think Antonia is kind of feral, too. It's in the Endless Mountains of Pennsylvania. It likes to hide from prying eyes, but if you show it a little love, it's decent.

When I graduated with an animal science degree, I found a job as a vet tech. I found a cheap apartment in a cheap town.

Aunt Karen had lectured more when I made my dutiful pilgrimage to see her after graduation. She blew cigarette smoke at her enormous flat screen, obscuring the evil face of a pseudo-psychologist who embarrassed people on television for money. "It's a scam. You'll see."

"It's not a scam. I know people from Pine Ridge. We were buddies in college."

That was a stretch, but Aunt Karen didn't need to know that. When I was a freshman, there was a gorgeous, adorable melanin-challenged couple, Sophie-Something and Jesse-Something Else. They were seniors, and already engaged. Because of the dismal size of Antonia's enrollment, seniors and freshmen were often in the same electives. We ended up in Literature of Ancient Civilization together, sitting in the back row during evening classes. (I worked afternoons at a little taco joint in town.) When we were forced to introduce ourselves during one of the weekly "Pair-and-Share" events the professor had coordinated to discuss Aeschylus and Enheduanna, I told them I was from Allentown, Pennsylvania. It turned out Sophie was from Philadelphia, making us practically neighbors. Jesse was from Pine Ridge, New York, right over the state line.

Sophie and Jesse made his town sound like a dream come true—friendly, little, full of beautiful people and places. They never mentioned how affordable it was, but when you're bored in class and you start looking up random crap on your phone... Well, I couldn't believe my screen.

Sophie and Jesse were planning to get their own place after graduation. They showed me some of the houses they were looking at one night when the antiquated overhead projector overheated and the professor insisted we all sit and wait patiently for it to cool off enough to come back to life.

That's right. I said two college seniors were buying a *house*. At first I figured one of them must've had money, but then a little more talking and a little more squinting at the phone revealed that Pine Ridge real estate seemed to be quite a bargain.

And if they could afford a mortgage, maybe I could afford to rent a room. Or even a whole apartment with a kitchen?

My other option was moving in with Aunt Karen, who had started telling me that I should try to find a "sugar daddy." Uncle Amir 2.0, or a town that sounded too good to be true? I was going to gamble on something that at least sounded like it wouldn't induce vomiting.

Aunt Karen was right there with me on the "too good to be true" part. While I packed the few items I had stashed in her spare room, she trailed after me, wailing in a voice that set off the neighbor's chihuahua. "That little hick town in the mountains sounds too good to be true. You've only been there for a weekend! This is a crazy risk, Lib-Lib. You should move in with me. You don't know *why* it's so cheap! I bet all the babies have birth defects! I bet it's near a nuclear testing site. A sewage station! A slaughterhouse!"

"I stuck around for the summer, Aunt Karen, but I have to go. My lease is signed. My job starts the second week of September. Look, if it's anything like you said, I'll move back. I promise." I may or may not have had my fingers crossed behind my back at the time.

Chapter Three: Libby

Where was I?

Oh, right. Aunt Karen, She-Who-Is-Hysterical. Despite ear-splitting pleas and the arrival of Renaldo or Rudolpho (some swarthy guy with chest hair that resembled roadkill) in his red Boxster, I tore myself away from Allentown and started my new life.

I moved to Pine Ridge in September. It's now January and I haven't seen any babies with two heads, haven't been exposed to sewage or radiation, and the only unreasonable expense is my coffee addiction. The Pine Loft takes a tenth of my paycheck, but I blame that on my own weakness and the fact that I pass the place on my way home from the clinic. I don't get out much, but I think Pine Ridge is perfect.

The only thing that would make it better would be a social life.

Oh, I go out with friends—sort of. It really is a small little town. I asked Dr. Peterson, my boss, if he knew of a couple named Sophie and Jesse, and he did. I looked them up and we've had dinner a few times.

Everyone is friendly, really.

But people seem... guarded or oblivious. Is that mean to say? I don't care, it's true.

There seem to be two kinds of people in this town. Group One includes people who will smile and chat, always super interested in you, but revealing only little, vague basics about themselves. Group Two includes people who smile and chat, talking a ton about themselves, but asking very little about me, the new girl.

I've decided, whether I'm right or not, that this bi-oddity (new word, go me) is because I'm new here. This is a tight-knit town, according to Jesse. (His last name turned out to be Smith.) I figure that people don't want to invest in me too much in case I leave and break their little hearts.

Well, I've got nowhere else to go, so I'm staying.

Sophie, who has only been here a few years longer than me, already seems relaxed. I've seen her in the store showing off their little boy, surrounded by a gaggle of old granny-types, looking like a queen with the heir to the throne.

Jealousy is a bitch.

I'm not jealous of Sophie! I just... I want a family. I want to *fit in*. I've been a loner for a long time, ever since I started realizing that the poor kids on food stamps with single moms don't *quite* fit in, no matter what the teachers said.

So, using the new pastel blue planner my boss had given me for Christmas (stuffed with gift cards to the bookstore, the sushi place, and The Pine Loft), I decided to change that. I had a planner. I was going to plan.

One foggy night last week, with Metallica's *Whiskey in a Jar* blaring as I savored my on-the-way-home cup of coffee, I opened the planner and actually looked at it.

It was pretty straightforward. There were spaces for monthly, weekly, and daily notations. I flipped past the first two weeks of January and discovered a Goals and To-Do Lists section. Dr. Peterson had even left me another present. "Oh, my gosh. I love my boss." Two vinyl sticker collections, both full of metal band logos from the eighties! I would have to ask him where he got such a perfect gift.

But back to the to-do list. I grabbed the matching baby blue gel pen that was stuck through a loop on the side of the planner and wrote:

Have a social life.
Stop living on coffee, cheese puffs, bananas, and sushi.
Find a club.
Get a date.

Chapter Four: Milo

There aren't any other minotaur families in Pine Ridge. The only female minotaur in town is my mother. When we traveled to Greece for my brother's wedding, there were gorgeous girls everywhere. Girl minotaurs, I mean.

I wasn't into them.

After the reception, my dad sat me down on the back of the private yacht my new sister-in-law's family had chartered. My father was a little tipsy. (It takes a LOT of ouzo and champagne to make a minotaur tipsy, in case you're wondering.) He asked me if I was into bulls instead of cows, and I told him no. Then he asked if there was someone back in Pine Ridge that had my heart. I told him no. He asked if I was one of those aromantic types, only he was slurring so it sounded like he asked if I was *aromatic*. After I sniffed at my suit for a few minutes, I told him I didn't smell like I'd bathed in anise, which is what drinking too much ouzo makes you smell like.

By that time, my mom came back on deck, looking for us. My father got this completely unhinged, lustful look in his eyes and started chasing her around the boat.

I was severely tempted to jump overboard and swim ashore.

The truth is, I'm probably one of the most romantic people I know—but no one else knows it.

Minotaurs have a thing for protecting and serving. Acts of service are our love language. I dream about having a wife I can protect and help. She'll look up at me adoringly. She'll be so small next to me that every time I'm around her I'll feel like I'm her living shield, a proud warrior—not just the guy who makes poison rings and recalibrates weaponized watches.

Yes, I said she'd be small next to me. Small and possibly on the helpless side. I admit it. I have a damsel in distress thing, but I'm not some neanderthal brute.

I blame history.

Pull up a chair.

My people were not always called minotaurs. We existed before that whole King Minos crap. We have been around as long as anyone else, human or "monster." Humans feared us, the same way they feared other half-man, half-animals. The peaceable taurosapiens pulled back into the shadows, forming secret rural communities. Every community had an underground lair equipped with escape tunnels and traps to prevent violent humans from attacking the clan.

And then King Minos found out that his wife had become friendly with a local blacksmith (taurosapiens like metal). The way my mother tells it, Pasiphae was nothing more than a friend to the smith, who she had commissioned to make armor for her oldest son, the Prince.

Minos, who was already two hammers short of a forge, decided she was having an affair and went on a murderous rampage, killing one of his own children. My ancestors of course then urged the queen and surviving royal children to take refuge with us.

Well, you know how it is when you're thrown together with someone day after day...

Yeah. Eventually, Pasiphae and Aspro (the smith) were secretly married and had a bunch of little half-human, half-taurosapien babies. And we started being called minotaurs. (I think we should have been called *Pasi*taurs. Why give that murdering idiot any credit? But you can't change two thousand years of history overnight.)

Ever since I saw the picture in mom's old history book, I've been a hopeless romantic. The picture is an old ink illustration that shows Aspro blocking the labyrinth entrance. His eyes are glowing red, his horns are glinting, and his nostrils are flaring. One hand holds a huge broadsword. The other arm is pushing Queen Pasiphae behind him. She's looking up at him with such utter love and adoration.

I want that. I want a woman I would die for and a woman who would be by my side, adoring me as much as I adore her.

That isn't going to happen in Pine Ridge.

There are two kinds of people here. One, there are people who know about the magical energies and entities who live here. They play it cool. They know that everyone isn't what they seem. They're all (99% of them) nice, normal-ish folks. What about the second group?

They are incredibly, stubbornly blind. They walk around with witches, wolves, succubi, and whatever else we have on tap, thinking that everything is normal. According to those people (all human), some of their neighbors are just a bit "eccentric."

The people in the second group would all be dead by dinner time if Pine Ridge weren't such a safe place to live.

Either way, I'm not going to find a woman who needs me here. If she's a vampire, a werewolf, or a witch, she'll be able to take care of herself and probably won't want me being my overprotective self. If she's a normal, oblivious human, she won't ever meet me. If she did, she'd run in terror, and that's no way to start a relationship.

Chapter Five: Milo

The Night Market opens at dusk, but the stall owners who can tolerate sunlight tend to come a little before so they can set up and not waste a single second of selling time.

Stalls are set up in a grid between the light poles in the lot. There are three rows. The ones closest to the street are run by residents who are human or who can pass for human. They also tend to sell stuff human "tourists" would buy, like crystals, fudge, hand-embroidered clothing, and more run-of-the-mill stuff. It's not any kind of "human-looking equals better" mentality, believe me. It was decided a long time ago, back in the fifties when the Night Market was first getting set up, that this arrangement would help the more "unique" vendors stay safe. After all, no matter how oblivious a human is, he or she will notice if you're about seven-feet tall and have horns coming out of your head. My stall is in the back row, the corner spot. It's a prime location.

Christmas, Hanukkah, Yule, Kwanzaa, and Solstice weren't too long ago, so there are still a dozen strands of multi-colored lights strung up between the poles. I think we should leave them up all year. It gives the market a bustling, festive air, and that's important in cold, foggy, mountain towns in January. Festive, fun places attract customers who want to browse. Otherwise, people go straight to the stall they need, buy their potion or bat wings, and get the heck back home to their nice cozy houses.

"Milo! Hey, man!"

"Leo! Good to see you! Back from touring, Mr. Big Shot?"

Leo is a werewolf who is also in a local band. (It's a pretty big deal in the NYC club scene, but he never brags. Actually, he rarely talks at all.) His wife is a witch. They're some of my best customers because they're part of the "Neighborhood Watch." It's not a full moon, so I don't hurry to put my silver-tipped goodies away.

The stocky, auburn-haired man grins at me. "Out again next weekend. We'll be gone for a solid week."

"Ah. Looking for something to fend off those city demons?" I start moving weaponry around, sliding choice pieces forward for Leo to see. Everyone knows violent demons love big cities. Their kills blend in and get blamed on drug dealers and gangs.

"Actually, no. I'm packing Robbie. What else do I need? Plus, Tessa and Charlotte will be with us."

I nod. The two-man band usually travels as a foursome, two sets of best friends, two couples. My heart stabs me in a way I wasn't expecting. "What can I get you, then?" I ask in a gruff, clipped voice that shocks the hell out of me.

Leo doesn't seem to mind. "Can you make me something pretty?"

I take out one of my tackle boxes. Tackle boxes are great for holding tiny tools and metallic parts like springs and screws. My boxes are covered with all kinds of band stickers. Skin Deep, the band that Leo is in with Robbie, another local (and vampire), has a fair amount of signage on my boxes. Leo sees the stickers and smiles.

"I gotta tip you better," he mutters, hands in his pockets.

"Well, I'd never say no to that." I have a black velvet drape on my table every night. Just because I'm showcasing deadly weapons doesn't mean I can slack on presentation. Right now, I clear a space and put down a selection of poison rings and some of my "daintier" weapons.

Leo looks at a black leather band that has a shiny silver box in the center. From the filigreed box came a knitting-needle thin dagger of shining silver. From the other side was a wooden rod of the same length and thickness with a silver tip.

"Don't trip." My voice is just a rumble in the dark, protective instincts nudging up in my chest. "The silver makes for easy penetration. The wood will slip right through the heart. It'll kill a vamp or a werewolf."

"Hell, that'll kill a human," Leo points out, never losing the half-grin on his face. "Anything in the heart, dude, beating or still. How does it work?" He lightly taps the center of the metal box with its ornate design.

"Telescoping barbs controlled by a catch on the band. It has a safety. The barbs resist pressure, however. An effective weapon that I can demonstrate." I bend down to my insulated lunch box at my feet and pull out a cantaloupe. I'm a vegetarian, and I usually eat one melon per night during my "lunch" break. If I get to use it as a demo first, that's fine. "Let's say this represents a human head."

"Let's say it doesn't. I believe you without puncturing an innocent fruit. How much?"

"Fifty."

"A steal. I'll take it. But can you make me something else, too? Something that isn't a weapon. A necklace?"

I flex my thick fingers, fingers that have a light coating of hair, the same as any bull. These mitts are big, but not clumsy. Still, I wouldn't consider myself adept at jewelry making. I've never really tried it unless it was to conceal a weapon. "There are two other stalls here that sell jewelry, Leo."

"Yeah, and they're both good places, but not what I want. I like your work. Your style. You put something of longing into the metal. Like a little piece of your soul, man."

I blink down at my wares. Really? My soul was in there? Maybe an occasional piece of hair, but... I shrug. Leo is a good customer and he doesn't talk much. That speech contained the most words I've ever heard him say at one time. If it means that much to him, I'll do it. "Sure, Leo. When do you want it and what did you have in mind?"

He hands me a drawing on a creased piece of staff paper. Two interlocking metal hearts, one covered with leaves and flowers, one covered with thorns and spikes. Leo and Tess.

Dang it. My eyes were instantly welling up. The wolf and his witch. My voice cracks, "Two weeks?"

"You're the best, Milo. You know, some woman's going to be so lucky when she finds you."

Leo walks off. I fold the paper carefully and hide it in my tackle box. I feel a tiny sliver of hope in my heart. When Leo speaks, it's important and he means it.

Lucky to find me.
I'll be lucky to find her, too...
Follow Milo and Libby as they find their way to a steamy happy ending!
Read *The Minotaur's Valentine* [1] today!

---

1. https://books2read.com/b/minotaursvalentine

Velvet Wings[1]

Lennox

I'm having a very bad day. No, let's make that a very bad month.

It's not enough to be one of the only mothmen left in West Virginia, or that I have no hope of finding a mate or even being able to pop into the grocery store without attracting terrified screams—but now my home has been destroyed, too.

With my forest gone and my career as an amateur arborist kaput, I do the unthinkable. I leave my family and head to paranormal-friendly Pine Ridge, knowing that I can find safety there...and maybe even get WiFi and the occasional convenience store veggie wrap. If I really want to shoot for the moon, perhaps in a year or two I'll be doing well enough to convince my hothead brother to leave the ruins of our old life and join me.

Cindy

I'm getting old. Okay, no, not really, but I'm becoming more *mature*. I just watched one of my best friends seize life with both hands and go from a struggling, single waitress to an engaged pastry chef and business owner. I want that. Okay, maybe I don't want to own a business, but I'm tired of random hookups and fun flings. I want to find my person, that one special somebody and Pine Ridge seems like the place to do it. I don't know what it is about this little town, but wedding bells always seem to be ringing!

---

1. https://books2read.com/velvetwings

There's just one problem. I'm not the good girl type. I don't know how to keep things serious. I don't even know where to *find* a guy who wants to settle down and start a new life. Even if I did, I don't know if he'd be into someone like me. (My friends say I'm kind of a lot.)

It's not like Mr. Sweet-And-Sensitive is going to fall out of the sky and land at my feet...

Chapter One: Lennox

I look at what's left. An army surplus blanket, one of my speckle-covered notebooks with a pen tucked inside, and whatever is in my old canvas book bag. I haven't even used it in months. I don't know if there's anything valuable inside.

Marlow hasn't fared much better. He has his leather Harley-Davidson vest, a tarp, and whatever he has in a big blue gym bag. His is probably better stocked. He travels more—which might be a blessing right now.

"Damn." Marlow looks at where we used to live. The lightning strike struck the biggest elm in the strand, and the bare trees, dry and tough from a historically dry winter, went up like matchsticks.

"It's gone. The whole strand. The whole woods!" My throat is full of tears. I don't care. It wasn't just home. It was my work, my hobby, my passion. It's not like anyone pays me to take care of the trees, but as a mothman, it isn't like I could go over to the West Virginia Department of Forestry and hand in my resume, either.

"Well. It's a big state. Spring is coming. Plenty of trees in the woods. Race you to see who can make a new nest!" My brother pounds me on the arm, his steely gray feathers at odds with my crow-black ones.

"Make a new nest? Here?" I shake my head, red eyes blinking back tears. "Marlow, no. This place isn't for us anymore. It's... stagnated. The humans know it, too."

Marlow's face is tight. "Humans are all idiots, and you know it. Let 'em leave. Then we'll rule the woods like we used to."

My antennae droop. My brother is the stupid kind of fearless. As our mother used to say, he's missing the bone in his head that tells him to avoid danger.

"We mothmen won't reclaim the area. The mining companies will move in. If not them, the mega marts and mall complexes. The new developments. Whether it's progress or purgatory, we're going to lose."

Marlow gives me a long, cold look before laughing. "You read too much, smarty wings. 'Progress or purgatory.' Ha. So what are you going to do? Make yourself your final cocoon and wilt away?"

I take a deep, patient sigh. Being the brains of the family (what's left of it) has some benefits. I'm used to dealing with Marlow's childishness. I've always been the mature "older brother" even though we're the same age.

"I think I want to go to a community that welcomes our kind."

Strong fingers tighten on my wrist before I can even cry out in pain. "You will not go to a CrossRealms, you idjit."

Whoo. *Idjit.* When the country drawl pours out like that, I know Marlow is close to losing his tough facade—and his temper.

"I'm not looking to fight evil vamps and demons! I like to prune trees, not whittle stakes. I was thinking someplace *peacefully* paranormal friendly."

Marlow snorts. "Not too many places around here like that. Thinking of crossing the ocean and hiding out in the Hebrides? I'd love to see you scrounge up money for airfare. Or did you plan on those wimpy little wings carrying you over the Atlantic?"

Yes. He's being a jerk. He's being a jerk because he's scared and upset. I try to remember that. I try to count to ten, but I can only make it to three before I snap out, "No! Like Moonlight Bay or Pine Ridge! Yeah. Pine Ridge. It's a little closer and a little warmer."

My brother's wings flare open, gray and red and angry. The markings on his wings are like eyes, black and crimson scowls on gray.

They're subtle enough that in the darkness of a moonlit night or a dense forest, humans just see flashes of shadow.

"You're going to leave our home? Coward! Deserter!"

Calm. Calm. Calm.

"There is nothing for us here. Come with me. Come with me and help me start a new home. We aren't going to thrive here. What happens when there's only one of us left? We just die out?"

"We'll meet someone. Someday."

"Out here, we're monsters. Up there, we'd be citizens. You know. Eventually." My antennae flatten down to my head, and my wings droop. Mothmen aren't social creatures. The idea of making friends and interacting scares me so much I could molt.

Marlow says nothing.

He knows I'm right. There is no chance of us saving our kind out here. No chance of mates. There are other mothmen and mothladies out there, scattered few and far between, but all of them have fled the cryptozoologists, crazy hunters, and curiosity seekers that have chased us to the edge of extinction and deeper into hiding.

Why have we stayed here in the wildest wilds of West Virginia?

I'm too scared to go.

He's too stubborn to leave.

What's more, Marlow isn't afraid to mix with people. Of course, he can only do it a few times a year, late at night during the huge festivals where they come to "celebrate" the mothmen most attendees don't truly believe in. People dress up like us (well, like bad imitations of us), watch grainy footage of turkey buzzards, and have parties. Marlow waits until these conventions have turned into bacchanals of monster fans and girls wearing tight tank tops with catchy slogans like "I'm Mad for Mothman" and "Mothman's Monster-Fudging Mate" and stuff like that. Then, he slips into the crowds. People love his "costume."

And if you believe his stories, those mothman chicks love it when he "keeps the suit on" while he satisfies them.

I would die. What if it was a trap? What if those girls find out it's not a suit and I end up dried and preserved on the world's biggest push-pin in the mother of all butterfly collections?

I'm dying right now, just thinking about making a move far from everything I've ever known, far from tradition, roots, and maybe...maybe someplace in this state, there's one of my kind that I haven't discovered yet. If I leave, I never will.

A shower of sparks and a loud crash startles both of us. Charred trees are crashing and falling like dominoes in the wind as drenching rain begins—too late to do any good.

"There is nothing left here," I repeat firmly.

"You are a quitter and weakling." Marlow glares.

"You aren't going to out macho me! If I don't 'quit' this place, our whole family will die out. Up there—there might be one of our kind."

"Like she'd pick you." He snorts, scoffing at my timid hopefulness.

"Yeah, I'm sure she'd rather have you, stud. Why don't you come with me? See what kind of mothman the ladies prefer?"

"Don't you try that dang smartass reverse psychology on me, Lenny."

"Don't call me Lenny. I hate that. And it wasn't reverse psychology, you idiot! That's what you do when you don't want the person to do what you said! I *do* want you to come with me! That was *bait*." I turn away in exasperation, my dark, solid black wings fluffed up in anger. "Hillbilly hick with wings."

A hard tackle takes me down.

"Heard that!"

As our home and world crash down around us, my brother and I fight in the wet mud, beating the tar out of each other until we're laugh-cry-cursing in the chilly late February air.

"Damn. Where was this rain hours ago when it would have saved us?" I shiver, wiping mud from my face.

Marlow lies next to me, panting. "I know, right."

We both sit there, getting drenched. It's the only way we'll get clean.

Finally, Marlow yanks me up. "Aw. Go if you want. Yankee."

"Don't you do that. You know we're not northern or southern. We're mothmen. Come with me, Mar. Please? I really don't want to leave you behind."

"Lenny." He heaves a deep sigh that ripples the feather-like hairs that make up our "fur." "If I don't stay, there won't be anything to come back to when you can't stick it up there in New York, with all those eight million people."

I wince like he landed a blow. "Eight million? Are you sure?"

"Heard it on the television in the back of the bait shop."

Another tree crashes, this one revealing an eerie orange glow. The fires are still burning, even in this wet, misty fog that's covering the mountain. Another lightning bolt sizzles the air, and we have nowhere to hide, no nests, no nothing—not anymore.

Unless I'm brave enough to make something new.

"I'm going. If I don't come back home by Christmas, you gotta come up there and find me, okay?"

"Deal."

We stand, awkwardly gathering our stuff as the rain starts to come down harder and faster. "Do we hug?" I ask, arms dangling like limp windsocks.

"You big sap."

But Marlow hugs me anyway.

Chapter Two: Cindy

"Ugh! Ugh! Ugh! Oh my God! Ohhhh. God!"

Will this loser please finish already?

Why do I keep doing this?

"Oh, yeah, baby! Who's your daddy?"

I'm glad I'm facing away from Frat Boy. Rolling my eyes while he's clearly giving his best pornstar-wannabe performance is probably rude. I don't answer his question. It's a turn-off. Hell, this whole night has become a turn-off.

It occurs to me that I'm doing a disservice to my fellow women. This guy is probably nineteen or twenty (old enough to be at the Pine Ridge campus of NYU), and he still doesn't know how to have good sex. He's rushed and clumsy, but he's not giving off "this is my first time" vibes. If I hadn't been soaking through my black fishnets since the moment I walked into the party a couple hours ago, his attempts at athletic fucking would be mildly uncomfortable. And he thinks outdated phrases like "Who's your daddy?" sound hot?

I am doing nothing for my fellow women in terms of training this bozo. That is probably rude—on my part.

And yes, having time to have deep introspective thoughts during passionate sex is also a sign that it's not good. Passionate is a misnomer.

Faking does nothing for either of us.

I pull away.

"H-hey!" Bozo is handsome enough, and yes, I know his name isn't Bozo. It's Brad or Bert or something. Right now, he looks like a stunned, breathless Adonis-in-training.

"This angle isn't working. You're not hitting my g-spot, you're totally neglecting my clit, and you didn't go down before moving right to home base. Also, 'Who's your daddy?' Ew, no. You don't know if I even have a daddy-kink. Which I don't."

Bozo blinks. "Well...You have a fat ass!"

"I know." I beam and pat my generously padded posterior. "And if you had been good, you probably would have gotten to fuck it on some future date. But this isn't a date. This is a party hook up, and I'm horny. Now, you'd better make me come, or I'm leaving. Want me to show you how?"

Bozo splutters. "I k-know how to have sex, skank!"

"Oh, God. Your poor, poor future wife. Learn to take directions." I pull my dress back down and leave whatever abysmal dorm room I'm in, walking past dozens of other couples who are spilling out of other rooms, making out in halls before they end for the night or take things inside and move to the next level.

As I get to the top of the stairs, a red plastic cup full of watermelon vodka splashes me in the back of the head.

I turn slowly. My lazy, psycho bitch smile spreads even slower. Bozo, holding up a pillow in front of his semi-adequate junk, gulps and slams the door shut.

Outside, I stand in the chilly mid-March air and let out a deep, guttural groan. It's more than sexual longing. It's sexual frustration. I slip into my car and roar away from the dorms.

Back at my apartment, I head into the shower with my favorite toy—but then stop as my phone buzzes.

Cathy: *Are you up?*

Cathy works at The River House restaurant. My fellow waitress is also my primary bestie. Claire, who used to be a waitress, is my secondary bestie. She's now my part-time boss. She and her almost-hubby own a bakery and coffee shop, and I help out when they have catering.

When the bakery side of the business opens, they've offered me a full-time job.

Cindy: Yes. Just had the most unsatisfying sex I've had in months. Called it quits, and now I'm getting into the shower with something long, thick, and suction-y.

Cathy: TMI

Cindy: Why are you up?

Cathy: How do we throw Claire a bridal shower without her knowing when she works at the place where we want to have it?

Cindy: This is what keeps you up at night?

Cathy: Also the plight of children in need, human suffering, and global warming. Oh, and the threat of nuclear war.

I put my head in my hand and nearly blind myself with my Octo-Pussy, my delightful teal tentacle toy.

Cindy: I'll ask Georgia to help. We'll say we're catering for some other person, but it'll be for her.

Cathy: But then she'll do all the work!

Cindy: It's late. I'm horny. I will have more plans tomorrow.

Cathy: Don't you ever want to find just one nice man to love and sleep with?

My heart hurts. Yes, I do. But I don't know if I can find that.

Cindy: Sure, but in the meantime, I'm keeping sex toy manufacturers gainfully employed.

Cathy: You're a mess and I love you.

Cindy: I love you, too.

Chapter Three: Lennox

Pine Ridge, New York.

Marlow acts like New York is a world away, but I just fly diagonally up Pennsylvania, spend the day hiding out-slash-napping in the mountains surrounding Antonia, Pennsylvania, and then work my way toward Pine Ridge. As the tractor-trailer drives, it's about seven hours. As the crow flies, probably five. As I fly—around six. (Crows don't worry if someone sees them. I do.)

In case you're wondering, no, mothmen do not have a fancy built in GPS in our antennae. I just took one of those complimentary folding paper road atlases from the Wheeling Travel Plaza, and then I darted down low enough to read road signs every now and again.

Sorry if it's not as mysterious as you thought—and you can see why I won't be putting my flying skills on display any time soon.

Once I get to the Binghamton area, my senses start to tingle in a way I've never felt before. Oh, maybe a flash here and there, but this time, it's like my whole body is lighting up from the inside out. Magic. Supernatural power. Paranormal beacons.

Ley Lines, in other words. Pine Ridge is a paranormal-friendly place because there are three intersecting Ley Lines. A supernatural powerhouse.

"I've gotta be close."

You would think that would spur me on, but it doesn't. I find a dense area of trees and land to have a quick pep talk and work on my hyperventilating.

What if I can't do this?

Marlow is right. I'm a coward. I'm timid. I'm shy. I'm...not good at things. I don't have skills. I mean—unless you have a sick tree. I'm good at woodlore, and I know a lot about plants. I know how to survive in the wild, on my own.

So why the heck did I decide to fly to a place where I'll need new skills I've never honed?

I wince as I see the sign in the glow of my red eyes, "Welcome to Pine Ridge, New York! The town with a heart as big as the great outdoors!"

Pine Ridge may be considered a small town to humans, but by loner in the West Virginia wilderness standards, it's intimidating.

Flying over it, my cowardly self-preservation instinct kicks in.

Well, Marlow *says* it is cowardly, but if I don't stay hidden, how will our species survive?

If I *do* stay hidden, how will our species survive?

"Six of one, half a dozen of the other," as my grandpa used to say.

There are thick snags and strands of pines everywhere in this town. I need to be near water. I want to be near enough to observe people and the magical beings who supposedly live among them.

Supposedly is a big, frightening word that makes me want to turn around and fly south, back home.

What if the rumors that trickled down over the past two centuries are just that? Rumors?

I decide to stay hidden until I have proof that Pine Ridge isn't just paranormal—it's paranormal-*friendly*.

I fly past the town, stomach churning as I see all the lights, and some are even scattered far into the hills. I'd like to fly further, but flying this many hours in two days, carrying all the stress of leaving home after watching it burn...

It doesn't surprise me when my body finally quits, wings fluttering limply until I touch down several miles from the last point of light, deep in a thicket of snow-covered boughs.

Cold, far from home, and alone.
Exhaustion and depression make a good sleeping pill.

Chapter Four: Cindy

"You look... tired."

Claire is polite and sweet and I love her. When I show up to help paint the bakery that will one day take the world by storm (Cakes by Claire, remember it), I don't look fabulous.

The only consolation is that I don't have work at The River House or classes today. Last night's failed frat party kicked off Spring Break.

"Why is Spring Break not even in spring?" I whine, grabbing a cup of the famous Cinnamon Streusel coffee that Claire and Georgia have gotten me addicted to. It's the perfect thing for a late February pick me up—especially if you're an idiot who barely got any sleep as you tried to chase a certain erogenous high that you just couldn't catch. "I can't afford to go to Florida, and I'm definitely not going home to Ithaca—they got thirteen inches of snow this morning! Whatever zany madcap fun I have will have to be around here."

"Ohhh, that explains why you look so beat. Late night Spring Break bash?" Claire pulls her long brown waves up into a red bandana and pulls on one of her fiancé's old white t-shirts.

Claire's honey is perfect for her, being a chef with a heart of solid gold—and ridiculously drool-worthy. Georgie is this gorgeous blonde Nordic-looking god with a chest like a whiskey barrel that worked out, and he's about seven feet tall. Even on Claire's very pumpkin-shaped physique, his shirt hangs loose like an old smock, becoming the perfect painting outfit.

"Not so much a bash as a crash," I say, pulling my own sandy blonde hair up into a sloppy bun. "You look like Rosie the Riveter's much hotter twin."

"Thank you! You look cute, too. Um. Are you sure you're up to painting?"

"Hey, I want the job as your assistant. The sooner this place is up and running, the sooner I can transition out of waitressing and into... something else. This, I guess."

"You don't sound very excited." Claire pulls out rollers and painter's tape, giving me a sidelong glance.

"No! I am! It's just that in three months, I'll graduate—after forever-and-a-half. This is my last Spring Break. Ten days of freedom before 'freebie' vacations are a thing of the past. I guess at twenty-five, it's about time."

"Hey, my timeline was the same—but for different reasons. I guess Georgie and I won't see you for a few days, huh? You'll be living it up—or laying low." Claire laughs with a wink.

I know she's probably picturing me having an endless loop of swinging singles' fun in my apartment or living at Jax Alley, which is a sexy-skeevy roadhouse bar outside of town. "Haha. No. Probably not much."

I don't want to tell Claire about how pathetic my love life has gotten. I'm supposed to be the sexy adventurous one, the one who is self-assured and brimming with confidence. Claire and Cathy don't look up to me, exactly, but they're the mild to my "wild." Claire wouldn't be happily engaged without Cathy and me. We told her to go for it and make a move when she met the hunk of hot chef who hides out in the kitchen.

I want that. Not necessarily the tall, beefy drink of water Claire has, but—

Oh, who the hell am I kidding? Yes, I want that. I want a big, strong provider and protector to wrap me in his arms and tell me that it's okay that I've putzed around with my life for so long and that I don't know what I'm doing. That it's okay that I don't know what to do with a freaking liberal arts degree, and who understands how much I dread moving back home just to be shunted along into my parents' plumbing business.

"I really do love working with you. I love working in catering, and I would be crazy not to stay here and help out in this bakery. With your flavors and designs, it's going to be big."

"Maybe. It sure popped In December and January when you helped out at Jan and Diana's wedding. We got lots of people lined up for tastings. If only we can get them to commit. If only we can get Cakes By Claire trending again once I actually have a bakery open and I'm not just working in Georgie's kitchen where the coffee shop prep takes up most of the space! And a website. And social media. Oh, God..." Claire puts her head in her hands.

"Hey! Hey, hey. You should worry about your wedding day, babe. Leave the social media and web stuff to Georgia and me."

"Oh! The catering department, too..."

"You. Georgie. Happily ever after. Wedding bells a-ringing. White dress. Fancy shoes. Tux."

"He'll be in a kilt." Claire looks glazed.

I go over and firmly take her hands. "Ooh. I like. I thought he had Viking blood."

"Orc."

"What?"

"No-rth! Northern Scotland. The Hebridean area," Claire stammers and stumbles over the words.

"Cool. Focus on that, okay? That's what really matters in life." I give Claire a big hug, expression pained where she can't see it.

Love and a lifetime partner. A passion to follow. That's what really matters.

Yeah, that's right. That's what I said. That's what I meant.

"You're right, Cindy. You're totally right. I've got the person I love most in this world, and we're getting married—and we have the money to make this place shine. We have the friends to help us. Oh, gosh. I'm going to start crying!"

I swallow a sigh and laugh instead as Claire hugs me and cries a couple of happy tears on my shoulder. I pat her back and roll my eyes heavenward.

No, not because this is a Hallmark moment.

Because I'm mad at myself.

Dang, I can dish out advice, but I sure as hell never learned how to take it.

Possessed By the Leonid King[1]
Felix Orbus Galaxy
Book One
Chapter One

"Felids shouldn't have been using them for food. They have far more value."

Rupex turned to face Marcus, a scrawny specimen of a Leonid with a scraggly, graying mane and slender paws more accustomed to manipulating data than the firing mechanisms on starcrafts or assault weapons.

"Only the poorest prides on the extreme outer rims eat humans. That's primitive nonsense. Probably just rumors." Rupex paced with a sickened sneer, his long tawny tail tapping on the floor of his craft as it swished between his black boots. Humans. Too stupid to negotiate with their betters properly. Selling themselves into contracts that spoke of "whatever service deemed necessary." Ha. Some Felids deemed a meal a necessary service of their employees.

"I've heard plenty of prides on the outer fringes do it. But if my data is correct—and it usually is—human females can be far more beneficial to our species as mates rather than meals." Marcus hurried forward, personal computing device outstretched. "Look. One minor chromosome booster delivered in the female's heat cycle makes human eggs compatible with Leonid sperm."

---

1. https://books2read.com/leonidking

Rupex paused in his pacing. A ripple of disgust ran down his spine, forcing his thick yellow-brown fur to a constricted stand under his protective black suit. "What... what *sickness* made you consider such an experiment?" Rupex demanded, his voice slick and threatening, a snarl in every word.

Marcus met his eyes over thick spectacles perched on his graying muzzle. "You know very well what sickness, Ru."

Rupex took a step back, eyes wide.

No one liked to talk about the Queen Fever.

SIX YEARS AGO...

Marcus spoke to Rupex and the rest of the crew, ten Queens and three Knights. Ru, as commander of the ship, was considered the King of the pride, at least until they docked and disbanded.

"I do not recommend we resupply at Tigerite-Three, sir. There are rumors of a contagious infection that doesn't respond to any treatment."

"This Queen flu? Males are immune, is that correct?"

"No, sir, it isn't that males are immune." Marcus' voice was suddenly thin and tight. "It's that males don't die. They get the fever, but it seems to pass harmlessly within a few days."

"Then why would it impact a female differently?" Silvia demanded, striding forward, her black uniform highlighting the magenta waves of fur that trailed down her neck. "That makes no sense."

"It could have something to do with the females' heat cycles. Males don't have them. When a female is in her heat—"

"Enough of the school cub lectures, Marcus!" Rupex quickly shut his medical officer down. "We need supplies. Only males will go on-world and get what we need. We'll be in and out of port in a day. Queens, males will quarantine on A-Deck. You will assign yourselves to rooms on B-Deck. There will be no fraternizing for the entire heat cycle, just to be on the safe side."

PRESENT

Rupex sat in his captain's chair and looked out at the sprinkled black and purple vista ahead of him.

Marcus had been right. Queen Fever did have something to do with heat cycles. And it was incredibly contagious. They'd soon realized there was only one option to prevent death once a Queen caught it—an immediate removal of her reproductive organs to stop the heat cycle that seemed to turn the fever into a lethal illness. Sometimes it was already too late. If her hormone levels had started to build, nothing could be done. Even injections of male hormones and prophylactic pills didn't fool the virus.

Within six years, most females of cub-bearing age had been sterilized. The only female Leonids who would be able to bear children were still children themselves. Girls who hadn't entered their first heat were safe.

"Now we have a vaccine, sir. But in the meantime..."

Ru nodded. People on certain planets complained about the population. They begged couples to cease reproducing with incentives and contraceptives. Ru had a special bitterness for those worlds. They had no idea what they were really asking for.

Imagine having no new births for six straight years aside from a rare litter here and there. And imagine most of the females of your kind disappearing within a few months of the disease breaking out. They'd only thought of surgery after the first few waves had swept through the Felix Orbus Galaxy.

The situation was desperate indeed.

"It would only be a temporary measure. I thought you ought to know. If we could test it here, I'd report my findings. It could be a stopgap solution, just until the younger generation of females matures."

"Hm," Ru answered with a single grunt, raking his paws through his dark, honey-colored mane. It wasn't that Leonid hybrids didn't exist. The Leonids were old-fashioned about their pride structures, but within the pride, interspecies couples were common. There were mostly Felix-Leonid couples, but in a few cases, the pairings were more unusual. Why, his own sister had raised eyebrows when she married a Canid from the Sirius Federation.

But that was for love.

And it was never with a human. Sapien planets (all measly three of them) still had the unevolved mammalian, avian, reptilian, and aquatic species. Human interactions with those species seemed to be permanently ingrained within most of them. They were unaccepting of different social structures. The ones he had met years ago still seemed to consider Leonids and Canids dumb animals they needed to condescend to, even while taking their money for trade and contracts.

There was the whole human "structure" to consider, too.

"Humans are so...furless. And weak. They're barely sentient. No Leonid in his right mind would want to mate with one."

"The chromosome modification would allow the Leonid genes to be dominant. Yes, the child would have some human characteristics, but they could be bred out in a few generations."

"No."

"A lighter coating of fur. No tail perhaps. Poor night vision. You know our evolutionary matrix crossed with a sapien at some point or else—"

"I said *no*, Marcus."

Marcus sighed. "Sir, I didn't want to bring this up, but this bulletin arrived from the Department of Health's senior officer at Serval-Five."

Ru snatched the screen Marcus was holding out.

"'Possible Queen Fever mutation linked to deaths aboard a Sirius Federation pleasure ship.' Bastet's whiskers!" Ru pushed the device back into Marcus' paws. "It's jumping species?"

Marcus made a mewing noise in his throat. "It could be. They'll know soon. They'll know how to treat it, too."

"But how could this happen now? It's been six... Oh." Rupex didn't finish his sentence. When Queen Fever first struck in the Felix Orbus Galaxy, interplanetary and intergalactic trade and travel had been halted in nearly all cases. It had opened up slowly this past year, now that the fever was almost eradicated and vaccinations were widespread.

The Serval planets were closest to the Sirius Federation.

He could add two and two together to create a very grim picture.

Marcus injected a note of hope. "Our vaccine will probably work on most mammalian peoples." He waited for a moment, a hesitant smile coming over his face. "And because of the structure of Queen Fever, it's not compatible with humans. Humans will be immune."

Ru groaned. He didn't like when Marcus was smug, but he might have earned the right this time.

Chapter Two

Layla paced. Boredom had finally latched onto her after ten days aboard the craft. At least she *hoped* it had only been ten days. Time seemed slippery in isolation. She was the only human on board, and she wasn't a passenger. She was *cargo*. She'd been sold by her no-good-not-even-boyfriend. A one-night stand gone horribly wrong on Sapien-Three, and now she was being sold as permanent help—or worse—to someone in the Felix Orbus Galaxy.

She'd heard rumors that the Leonids ate humans like humans ate the unevolved cows and pigs. She also heard that Leonids were a proud race who despised humans. They didn't want them around, so maybe they'd be just as happy to let her work off a passage back to Sapien-Three, where she would track down Paul Bermauger and ship *him* to the other end of the solar system.

"Miss Human?"

Miss Human. At least her captor was polite. And to give him credit, it wasn't his fault that she was cargo. You could buy hired help legally anywhere in the galaxy, although the beings being bought were supposed to do the negotiating and bartering themselves, like a modern form of indentured servitude.

"Yes, Mr. Lion?"

"Mr. Leonid, please. Miss Human, you are being taken to a human clearinghouse on Lynx-Nineteen. Was that your intention?"

"No. I was hoping for something on Sapien-Three." She was hoping for anything, anywhere, honestly. A human without an elevated degree or a family had pretty crummy prospects. "Actually, I was hoping not to be on this ship at all, at least not in the cargo bay!"

The old lion-dude crept forward. She could see him now. She usually only heard his voice on the intercom making sure the service droids had delivered adequate food and water. Her "cell" was the size of four bunks pressed together and twice as wide. It had a bed and a minuscule shower/waste removal unit, a sink, and a media viewer. Of course, all the shows were from the Felix Orbus Production company, but still... She was getting into shows like *Pride to Pride* and *Cubs Say the Strangest Things*.

She'd seen pictures of Leonids back on Sapien-Three, her home planet. They were huge, usually about seven-feet tall with lashing tails and manes the size of a walk-in closet. This guy reminded her of her hopeless fourth-grade math teacher, who had finally given up on teaching and let them play games on their comms all year. He had the same air of wizened exhaustion to him, even if he did tower over her through the partition.

"Could you clarify, Miss Human?"

"Layla. Miss Layla, Mr. Leonid. I said I'm not supposed to be in your cargo bay."

"Why not? That is the usual way humans travel aboard off-world ships on long journeys when they haven't paid a passenger fare. If you only pay cargo rates, this is what you get. You have adequate space to sleep and eat."

"Yeah, but I'm not supposed to be cargo! I wasn't even planning to go off-world!"

The shaggy gray brows shot up and got lost in wispy gray fur. "You didn't negotiate your own contract?"

"No. I'm trafficked. I told you that."

"You did not! You most *certainly* did not! Leonids do not hold with slavers. What your owners do with you once you're paid... that's their business. But a subject must negotiate their own purchase. Sweet

Bastet." He flapped one paw to his cheek and knocked his own glasses off.

Layla tried to remember the first few days on board the ship. She had been drugged out of her mind and sleeping a lot. That wasn't their fault, that was Paul-the-Wonder-Slug's fault. *Maybe I dreamed I had a conversation. Or maybe I did have it, but I slurred so badly that I made no sense.*

"Miss Human, our craft is not going to Sapien-Three, or even out of the Felix Orbus Galaxy. I can arrange for someone to refund your purchase price to Lynx-Nineteen."

"Good luck."

"Yes, well... That's only one small problem. Here is another. You *are* cargo on our vessel. You are listed on our manifest. Your passage was paid as part of the contract price. With the contract refunded, you owe us passage fees."

"Good luck getting that, too. I'm broke. I would negotiate a contract with your captain if he needs someone to cook or clean. I'm good at those things." Layla leaned against the glass partition between her accommodations and the rest of the ship, hoping Leonids couldn't smell liars. She could clean just fine. Cooking was a work in progress, but you had to have food and a heat source at the same time to practice.

"I have another proposition for you. It's much easier work. All you have to do is hold still."

RU SAT IN HIS QUARTERS. As captain and owner of the ship, his quarters were the biggest and best—but they weren't much in the way of luxury. Once, he would have gone in for all that finery, but new jade carvings or silk sleep hangings didn't mean much anymore. One concession to luxury was the bejeweled frame that held Silvia's picture. It mocked him as he looked at it from his empty bed, and he put it hastily away. He didn't like to look at those laughing eyes, didn't want to imagine her bold voice or her flirtatious purr.

He'd missed his shot there. A captain wasn't supposed to fraternize with his requisitions officer, even if he was King of the pride. He'd planned to ask her about a courtship once her year aboard was officially up for renegotiation.

Well... speaking of shots to take... he could use a shot of Leonid homebrew right now. Or even one of those weak little human cocktails.

Marcus was going to ask the only remaining human in the hold, a female, if she'd like to transfer her contract to the crew of the *Comet Stalker*.

The crew was currently Marcus and himself. Marcus had already made it clear that he would be having no part in this experiment. He was much older, and he assumed his sperm viability wasn't the best. That meant this insemination business was up to him.

"But I'm not ready to be a father!"

That wasn't exactly true. With cubs being in short supply and almost every planet seeming like a motherless wasteland and Queens being all graying or young kits...the idea of family danced through Ru's dreams on a regular basis.

It's just like paying for a surrogate, Ru tried to reassure himself. Some wealthy Leonids had done that, paying for a female who would enter her first heat in a few years, booking her womb for a litter in the future.

Gods, what desperate times.

Marcus knocked on the sliding hatch to his room, then entered the access code without waiting for a reply.

"I told the girl she would perform a personal service for you. I didn't specify what. I figured you'd prefer to tailor your explanation to your tastes. By the look on her face, I think she suspects it's at least a bit sexual in nature." Marcus gave Ru a guilty nudge.

"But it isn't. This is medical. Why didn't you tell her the precise nature of your 'experiment'? You'll be the one who collects my *contribution*—well, not personally," Ru preferred not to use the anatomical terms at the moment considering his shock, "and sees that it manages to find its way into the correct receptacle. Right?"

"Inject? Oh, goodness. No. You see, humans don't give off visible signs of heat. Their body temperatures may not even elevate! It happens once a month, in a two-day window, but it can come early or late. Many things can influence it, too. Diet, stress, exercise, weight—"

"Marcus, spare me the lecture. What are you saying?"

"I'm not a doctor of reproductive science. I'm a medical officer with a new hobby, thanks to this terrible disease we've lived through. I'll do my part and research the most expedient method of conception between a human female and a Leonid male. That's how I can help. If *you* want to help the Leonid population, you're going to have to do this the old-fashioned way. Mate the girl every day for a month, or thereabouts."

"We'll be docking in two weeks! We're picking up a new crew at Leonid-One!"

"It's a simple enough matter to get word to the crew you've hired that they'll still be paid and they'll have two weeks initial leave. I can assign them tasks. We have an entire bay that's unfilled. Set them to acquiring cargo. Besides... if the outbreak aboard that Sirius vessel *is* a mutation of Queen Fever, all ports except designated survival ports will be closed for a month or two."

Ru hung his head in frustration, a growling groan echoing in the large, domed captain's quarters. "That a Leonid should lower himself..."

"Maybe humans aren't the intellectual planetoids you think they are. I spoke to the cargo today and found her competent."

"The *cargo*. The fact that they ship themselves as cargo and not passengers—"

"Because they're poor, Rupex. Their planets are longer established and more decimated by war and want, yet most stubbornly refuse to even leave Sapien-One, the original Earth." Marcus' nose twitched, and his tail did a nervous pit-pat on his ankle.

Marcus had been with Rupex for the last seven years. The grizzled old lion had been the only one to stay with him through the Grounding when all starcraft were only allowed to dock on their original home worlds or their designated survival ports. This wasn't necessarily by choice—medical officers were in critically short supply and every ship was now required by law to have one or have their ship's registry rejected. Ru didn't always enjoy Marcus' company, and the ship was large enough to allow them to avoid one another on most occasions. Still, Ru knew him well enough to recognize the signs of impending bad news.

"What is it?"

"What's what?" Marcus avoided his eyes.

"Your tail is *fluttering*. Don't tell me. The mutation has been confirmed to be Queen Fever?"

"Oh. No. I haven't heard one way or the other. It'll probably be a day before they send a new bulletin. No, it's about the cargo. The girl."

"Girl? A cub!"

"No, no. A woman. A young lady named Layla. She wasn't intending to go to Lynx-Nineteen."

"I hope not. They'd eat her. That's an almost entirely primal backwater."

"She was sold. As in, someone sold her. She didn't negotiate her contract."

Ru's mane bristled out and his claws unsheathed in rage. "What? *What*!?"

"Calm down."

"I will not! You volunteered to take over the cargo assignments while I was down with the post-vaccination reaction! I leave you in charge for two days and you take on a trafficked human? Manes and tails, Marcus! We're going to be permanently grounded for this!"

"I picked the cargo up from a vessel that wasn't going to the outer reaches of the Felix Orbus. I didn't know she wasn't moving of her own volition, Rupex. She was asleep, which is standard for most humans on a galaxy jump. Nothing twigged my suspicions, and I hope you won't pretend she would have aroused yours, either. You've been on autopilot since—"

"Quiet. That's an order."

Silence filled the deck. They both knew what Marcus would have said. Rupex had been on autopilot, functioning automatically since he lost his sisters and the Queens of the *Comet Stalker*. He took on skeleton crews and long-haul freights that would keep him on his ship for as long as possible. Planets within the Felix Orbus Galaxy seemed permanently touched by death and sadness, with a dearth of cubs and Queens, and many citizens (especially on the smaller and more distant planets) were claiming they should either remain in isolation or revert to feral states to cope with the new reality.

"The stars feel familiar." Rupex double-checked the navigation settings and the alerts before stalking away.

"Ru... We're not going to rebuild without change. Do you want to stay stuck in the past, where we were helpless? Or do something to fix it?"

Rupex had to get away from Marcus before he clawed him. He could feel the dagger-like tips of his claws passing through the soft sheath of his paws. There was no fixing this.

But maybe the older Leonid has a point.

Somehow, someway, he would have to move forward. The *Comet Stalker* could jump galaxies, but it couldn't travel back in time.

Chapter Three

Layla felt smug. And worried. And irritated. Whatever that emotional blend was, she wanted to patent it and sell it.

Instead, she was going to sell herself to some alien cat-man.

The idea of selling her services, whether it was having sex or cleaning a bunker didn't bother Layla. Growing up poor on Sapien-Three meant that you were always looking for any way to make cash. That was one reason she hadn't struggled too hard when she woke up in the hold of some strange vessel. Part of her had been relieved when she realized the accommodations were clean and the food was good and plentiful. Another part of her, while still worried, had been curious about what kind of contract she'd been sold into. A contract meant money, or at least food and shelter.

She hadn't known until she'd explored the media viewer and the limited number of books that she was on a Felix Orbus craft. Most people from the Sapien planets preferred to stick close to their three human-friendly rocks. Those who did leave didn't usually go to the Felix Orbus planets. Layla wasn't sure why. But in the last handful of years, ever since she'd been forced to start looking out for herself, she hadn't met anyone who'd been to that galaxy. The smug feeling was the most comfortable, so Layla tried to hold onto it while she paced in her little room.

Ha. Leonids, Servalis, Lynxians, and Tigerites were so aloof. So stand-offish. They wouldn't dream of coming to the Sapien planets. They weren't at any of the Galactic Games that she could remember.

But here I am, taking up space, and we're weeks away from wherever we're supposed to land, and what does the big horny lion-man want to do?
She didn't know.
Curiosity came back. *Maybe he just wants a good belly rub?*
It wasn't that interspecies dating wasn't a thing—it just wasn't *her* thing. On Sapien-Three, interspecies couples were rare and were usually just there for refueling. She could count on one hand the number of interspecies couples she'd met personally.
He doesn't want to be a couple. He's probably bored and doesn't have a sex droid. The first one pays for my passage and the rest he can pay for with cold, hard credits.
How much should she charge?
Her friends who traded in carnal pleasures usually asked for a thousand credits or more per exchange, but they were *good* at it. They were professional seductresses with skills and moves.
Layla didn't even have a dress. She had the black blouse and faded jeans she'd been wearing on her date and a simple white robe that came with the clean linens the service droids brought every day.
They're clean. Everyone says cats are clean. It'll probably be basic in-and-out stuff.
I wonder if they have fur on their—
"May I enter?"
Layla jumped off her bed so fast that she stumbled and smacked into the glass partition. That wasn't the little old lion-man. This was a different voice, deeper and...wider somehow. It was almost like a different frequency, radiating in her ears and sliding down to rest in her middle.
"Yes. C-come in." She tried to lean seductively against the edge of the bed, praying he hadn't been watching her on some corridor camera to witness her spectacular burst of clumsiness a moment ago.
The being who stepped up in front of the glass partition was easily seven feet tall. He wore a black suit that looked like it might be a cross between silk and leather, which Layla recognized as Thermagyle, a

polyblend of fabrics recommended for extended time in space because of how it adapted to temperature changes and gravitational force fluctuations. Above the suit, which seemed to consist of a tight, chest-hugging shirt and fitted trousers, was a massive head.

A massive head with dark golden eyes spanning a wide feline nose, rounded ears perched above hard brows, and a tawny, brownish-yellow mane that flowed past his shoulders.

Thoughts spilled into her brain.

Tall.

That head! It's huge.

I wish I had hair like that. I wonder what conditioner he uses?

"Miss Layla?" The voice that rumbled out was businesslike and disdainful.

Layla nodded, her entire perspective changing. *Nope. This is not a sex call. This is a "Will you kindly attend to returning my communications and hanging up my suits?" deal.*

"I am Rupex, King of this pride, captain of the *Comet Stalker*. Welcome aboard as a passenger." He pressed one paw to a panel on the side of her chamber.

The glass vanished with a whooshing shift, sliding up into the ceiling. Layla was staring at his paw. It was the size of her head, thick and furry with light brown pads. She wondered if Leonids still had claws, and when did they use them if they weren't typically on display?

"I am Layla Threewood. Domestic and retail worker. Personal services provided based on a contract-by-contract basis." Layla hoped she sounded professional and polished, keeping her eyes locked on the Leonid's face. She refused to look away, even though she was growing twitchier inside with every passing second. Leonids were supposed to be as intelligent as humans, maybe even more so... but when she looked at those golden eyes with oval pupils, she felt like she was looking at something incredibly foreign and wild, something lost and intimidating.

Rupex nodded. "Would you like to move your quarters to A-Deck? It's usually for crew, but we are currently en route to pick up our new crew."

That would explain why she hadn't seen other people milling about or heard other noises and voices on the ship.

"Sure. Thank you. Better than being considered 'cargo.'" She knew her tone had dipped into the "sassy" category by the way Rupex's eyes glinted and his massive muzzle, which was somehow flatter and more human than what she remembered from the pictures of lions she'd seen in old books about earth animals, scrunched up to reveal long white canines.

"You humans are the ones who book yourselves off-world and sell yourselves to the highest bidders, making yourselves 'cargo.'"

"I didn't. And do you know how weak Sapien credits are when compared to most other galaxies? Sometimes it's the only way we can afford to get off-world and travel to a place where we can get a job. Cargo or starvation. Hmmm." Layla held up both hands and pretended to weigh the options. "I know you Leonids wouldn't understand that. You stay in your own galaxy and keep with your own kind, right?"

Yes, she was being a brat, but his tone had touched a nerve—and so had the mention of her poverty. Sapien-Three had once been the jewel of the solar system. No more.

"Keep to our own kind? Stay in our galaxy? Wh-what *ignorant* rock have you been hiding under for the last decade, human?" Rupex spat the words like a vile curse.

"Excuse me? Ignorant? Ha! They were right about Leonids. You're all proud—jerks." Layla substituted the word quickly for the less offensive option. Those teeth were big, and that mouth... He could probably bite her arm off in one nip.

Rupex curled his fists. She could see the tips of claws now, dark, sharp, and short. "Queen Fever, fool. Heard of it?" Rage was practically sweating out of him. His fur bristled, and his whole form seemed to swell.

There was a line here. And I crossed it.

"Nn-no?"

"Wait? No?" The anger didn't dissipate, but it was suddenly coupled with confusion. "Are you joking?"

"No! We don't even have queens on Sapien planets. We're all democracies. Or worse."

"A Queen. A female Leonid or Felid of cub-bearing years. Queen Fever raged for over two years, killing almost every female from fourteen to fifty."

Layla could tell when she blushed. She could also tell when all the blood vanished from her face. "Oh my God. Like the Maximus Virus in 2800?"

"Yes, except that ours was deadly only to Queens. Something to do with their hormone levels." The Leonid looked away. "Millions died. Millions more sacrificed their ability to have cubs to stave off the disease. Some wealthy families in the Felix Orbus Galaxy actually went so far as to 'reserve' the reproductive services of young female cubs who wouldn't mature for years in advance, hoping to have offspring of their own later."

Layla felt a drizzle of warmth for the big beast who was now pacing in a perfect line, turning in sharp right angles at the end of the walkway in front of her former quarters. "I'm so sorry. I honestly didn't know. I didn't get to sit down and hear about the intergalactic news and affairs growing up. I was in survival mode, just like your people were. The reasons were different, but the struggle was real."

The hulking figure in black paused in front of her long enough to nod and then paced away again. "Poverty is a greater problem on Sapien-Three because humans are reluctant to innovate and trade with other mammalian species."

"And we have a shitty environment, corruption, war, and disease. But sure, blame the stubborn jackoffs who won't buy cheap groceries from the interspecies couple down the street."

A growl that rippled the air around her made Layla bite her tongue.

They could eat you, you know. Or just kill you. Starve you in that little glass cell. They could do all of that, and no one would ever know.

No one would ever care.

"Reasons aside, Leonid credits exchange at eighteen to one with Sapien credits."

Layla blinked. "That much? Damn. Never mind. Take me to the kitty planets."

Rupex slammed a paw to his forehead and squeezed his eyes shut. "Kitty planets? No. No, this is pointless. Worthless. Insane. Goodbye, Miss Layla. I will prepare quarters for you and hope your stay is comfortable. We will find a ship to take you to a planet where you can negotiate a contract for your services."

"But I thought the little old lion-man said *you* wanted my services!" Layla protested, the sound of credits inflating her pitiful account drowning out the irritation and woe in his voice.

"That was before I talked to you!" Rupex pushed a button on the wall and it lit up, showing a warm green light under the pads pressing it down. The silvery panel of the wall slid up, and he was gone.

www.ingramcontent.com/pod-product-compliance
Lightning Source LLC
Chambersburg PA
CBHW071110060226
39286CB00019B/246